LAZINESS IN THE FERTILE VALLEY

ALSO BY ALBERT COSSERY
AVAILABLE FROM NEW DIRECTIONS

———

A Splendid Conspiracy
The Colors of Infamy

ALBERT COSSERY

LAZINESS IN THE FERTILE VALLEY

Translated from the French by William Goyen

Foreword by Henry Miller
Afterword by Anna Della Subin

A NEW DIRECTIONS BOOK

Manufactured in the United States of America
Published simultaneously in Canada by Penguin Books Canada, Ltd.
New Directions Books are printed on acid-free paper.
First published by New Directions as *The Lazy Ones* in 1949.
Reissued as a New Directions Paperbook (NDP1265) in 2013.
Design by Erik Rieselbach

Library of Congress Cataloging-in-Publication Data
Cossery, Albert, 1913–2008.
[Fainéants dans la vallée fertile. English]
Laziness in the fertile valley / Albert Cossery ; Translated from the French by William Goyen.
pages cm
ISBN 978-0-8112-1874-0
I. Goyen, William, translator. II. Title.
PQ2605.O725F313 2013
843'.914—dc23   2013027463

10 9 8 7 6 5 4 3 2 1

New Directions Books are published for James Laughlin
by New Directions Publishing Corporation
80 Eighth Avenue, New York 10011

CONTENTS

FOREWORD

Albert Cossery is a young Egyptian, born in Cairo, who spent a number of years in Paris and writes his books in French. He is rapidly gaining recognition not only in the French-speaking world but in England and soon, we expect, in America. All his books have been translated into Arabic and are creating a stir in the Near and Middle East. They are destined, in my opinion, to be translated into many tongues, for their appeal is universal. He writes exclusively about the unalleviated misery of the masses, about the little men, the forgotten men—men, women and children, I should say—forgotten of God. No living writer that I know of describes more poignantly and implacably the lives of the vast submerged multitude of mankind. He touches depths of despair, degradation and resignation which neither Gorky nor Dostoevsky has registered. He is dealing, of course, with his own people, whose misery began before Western civilization was dreamed of. Despite the seemingly unrelieved gloom and futility in which his figures move, the author nevertheless expresses in every work his indomitable faith in the power of the people to throw off the yoke. Usually this hope is voiced by one of the characters apparently without hope. It is not a shout which is given forth but a quiet, determined affirmation—like the sudden appearance of a bud in the darkest hour of the night.

Cossery gives tongues to the speechless ones. Naturally, they do not speak like the professional agitators indoctrinated with Marxism. Their language is childlike, simple to the point of foolishness, but pregnant with a meaning which, when understood by those in power, will cause them to tremble and shudder. Often they express themselves in fantasy, a dream language which, in their case, demands no psychoanalytical interpretation. It is as clear as the handwriting on the wall. In effect, this is precisely what Cossery is doing—writing his message on the wall! Only, he is not speaking for himself but for the multitude. He does not revel in the horrors of misery, as might be imagined from a cursory glance; he is heralding the coming of a new dawn, a mighty dawn from the Near, the Middle and the Far East.

His books are saturated with a mordant, savage humor which makes one laugh and weep at the same time. There is no separation between the author and the pitiable figures he depicts. He is not only for them, he is of them too. In expressing their vagaries, one feels that Albert Cossery is also just learning to use his voice, to use it in a new way, a way that will never be forgotten. To a Westerner, especially an American, his types will probably seem outlandish and ridiculous, almost incredible. We have forgotten that men can sink so low; we know nothing of this abysmal level of existence, not even in our most backward regions. But I am assured by those who know that there is nothing the least incredible, the least fantastic, about Cossery's creatures or their situation. He has given us a reality all too real, incredible only that in such an "enlightened" era such things can be.

HENRY MILLER, 1945

LAZINESS IN THE FERTILE VALLEY

I

The child loaded his slingshot, held his breath, and aimed carefully. Then he fired with his head thrown back and his mouth open, his whole face shining with a strange excitement. The rock flew like an arrow, whistling, and disappeared in the branches of the sycamore. All the birds flew away with little cries of fright. He had missed.

Serag remained motionless, standing on the embankment that bordered the field of corn. He had been watching the child—a boy of ten, full of violence, with immense bulging eyes and the face of a precocious murderer. He was dressed in rags and seemed to have come from very far; his whole person bore the marks of adventure. Serag was fascinated by his ardor, and also by a certain extravagance that emanated from him. He behaved, really, in an astounding manner, lavishing his energy in jerky movements like a mechanical toy. From time to time he bent down to pick up more rocks, then bounded up to shoot his slingshot again. He shot now without aiming, stone after stone, as if seized with panic. Serag noticed his short quick breathing, like panting. He couldn't keep himself from watching, smiling foolishly at this exasperated violence which seemed, in the solitude of the fields, like a terrifying nightmare.

How long had it been going on? Serag remembered having seen the child; then, abruptly everything had changed. He didn't know what this change consisted of: it was everywhere in the air like a palpable anguish.

He thrust his hands in the pockets of his pants, straightened his shoulders a little as if to fortify himself against this blind frenzy; then, again, he became immobile, attentive to the least gesture of the child.

The sycamore stood just ten steps from him, on a side of the path where the mass of its branches made a wavering shadow. The path ran across the corn field and rejoined the main highway. Only a part of the highway could be seen and, bordering it, a yellow villa with green shutters which was silhouetted against the somber blue of the sky. Sometimes a car passed at high speed, leaving behind it a long track of dust. And sometimes a mule cart lumbered lazily by, taking an infinite time to disappear. But at this moment the road was deserted.

The child still pursued his hunting with fury. He struggled, ruthless and determined, menacing the entire universe with his slingshot till the countryside rustled with the secret alarm of his anger. He was irritated at his own clumsiness, and uttered obscene curses between his clenched teeth. From time to time he stopped and with a suspicious glance surveyed the few birds that were still hidden in the branches of the sycamore. Then he took up his hunt with redoubled energy. He seemed to see nothing around him, entirely absorbed as he was by his frantic excitement.

Serag felt himself frighteningly alone in the countryside with this terrible child armed with his slingshot. He began to feel an acute uneasiness, almost a madness. He would have liked to flee, to escape the spectacle of this frenzy, whose danger he measured by his own horror and helplessness. But he didn't dare to move. His limbs were completely paralyzed, his mind strangled by fear. A terror of delusion overwhelmed and tortured him. This was an unending punishment. At each movement, at each gesture of the child, he felt again a violent pain in his neck that seemed to last an infinity. Without realizing it he lowered his head, bit his tongue and stiffened all his muscles so as not to succumb to dizziness. Soon tears came to his eyes, and he began to cry gently, heedlessly.

With an effort he turned his head and threw a despairing glance around him. An implacable and weird solitude dominated all the countryside. It was the unchangeable Egyptian countryside, with its fields of corn and sugar cane, congealed in a distressing torpor. Everywhere the earth was at rest, flat and monotonous, giving no sign of life. In the distance, through the light haze, he could see the shapes of date trees, their slender trunks balancing their palms like giant fans. The ditches mirrored the lazy water in silver reflections of the sun. Suddenly, from the depth of the horizon rose a flight of crows; they hovered for a moment in space, then dispersed in the shifting crevices of the sky. Serag looked to the side of the road. At first he could see nothing; then a woman in a black dress passed slowly, an urn balanced on her head. He couldn't see her very well, but she was moving in the distance, a living thing, and it comforted him.

The sun was scarcely visible behind the heavy clouds which pursued it continuously. It was a winter sun, an artificial sun, brilliant but without warmth. From time to time a cold wind swept all the expanse of the fields, making the tall stalks of corn undulate. The whole countryside seemed roused, as if by a wave, then calmed little by little, returning to its gloomy desolation. Once more Serag looked at the child. This time he felt a shock in his chest. His legs gave way under him as though they had been cut. The child continued his hunt with increased frenzy. It was no longer a human thing; it was as though a demoniac force were attacking the void with fury. Serag looked at the boy without believing in him. He was seized by an imperative need for sleep. But how to sleep before this absurd and annihilating vision? At bottom, the thing that terrified him the most in this mad agitation was the mystery that it seemed to conceal—the mystery of a monstrous universe, filled with men overwhelmed by work and succumbing under the strain. He couldn't be wrong about this. Serag recognized in the child's insane frenzy all the signs of a labouring and trapped humanity. Never before had the world of men dedicated to slavery struck him with this strange force. Could it be a sign from destiny? Seized by a superstitious fear, Serag waited, his heart pounding, as if on the threshold of an ultimate revelation.

Serag had heard that men worked, but these were only stories that one told. He had never believed them completely. He himself had never seen a man work, outside of those futile and ridiculous employments which for him had absolutely no value. However, for a long time he had felt the desire to see one of those men who worked arduously with their hands, and who carried the stigmata of painful labour. But it was very difficult for him to do this; he knew of no practical way of meeting them. Ever since he had looked for work, he had tried in vain to find them. At home his family considered him a fool and a dangerous maniac. When he spoke to them of his wish to work, they all showed incredulous faces, not only because of his decision, but rather from a lack of understanding. This passed their comprehension. Serag didn't know whom to ask for help. All the people he knew devoted themselves to various fruitless, insignificant tasks which had nothing in common with true work. Those among them who perhaps participated in some rough and painful labour never showed it. They always seemed to hide this pain within themselves, like a shame or a remorse. Serag had had unbelievable difficulties with this problem. With all his soul he wanted to approach some men at their work so that he might know what it meant.

But was this enraged child a worker? Certainly he had neither the walk nor the appearance of one. If all the men who worked drove themselves like this, life would no longer he possible. And only to chase birds! What then when he worked in a factory! For Serag could only conceive of serious work in the inspiring atmosphere of machinery in action. He had a completely romantic idea of the operation of a factory. He was awed by the grandeur of work accomplished in common by thousands of men. But for this, all jobs seemed to him completely insignificant—equivalent, almost, to doing nothing. However, whatever the child was doing did not even correspond to these phantom professions. Serag tried to decide in which category of workers he belonged. But the child's behavior escaped all classification; his efforts seemed to go beyond the limits of human endurance. He no doubt obeyed some obscure design; he belonged to a sort of desperate and fallen humanity, more tenacious in its battle for subsistence. Serag had never seen anything like it. He found his whole conception of the world shaken.

He was seized by a deadly apprehension and asked himself how all this would end. Was there no one to stop the child? He could no longer hold his rigid position; his numbed legs had grown heavy, like a mass of lead. He had cramps in his stomach. He clenched his teeth so as not to cry out, leaned his head toward the ground and felt he was going to vomit. He closed his eyes, reopened them painfully, yawned, made a gesture of enormous weariness, then let himself fall, exhausted, on the edge of the bank. A moment later, he took a piece of bread from his pocket and began to chew it. He had just remembered that he had eaten nothing since he had risen.

A green and white car passed on the highway, honking repeatedly, as if sending out a message of distress. The noise resounded in the countryside, dying out slowly and leaving an impression of uneasiness. Serag watched the child shoot his last rock with a feeling of deliverance. What would he do now?

The child hesitated a long moment, giddy and breathless. Then with the back of his hand he wiped the snot that dripped from his nose, sniffed noisily, raised the front of his rags and minutely examined his sex; then he leaned his back against the trunk of the sycamore. He seemed beaten by his frenzy which had ended in nothing. Suddenly he saw Serag and a gleam of surprise kindled in his eyes and illumined his face streaming with dirty sweat. He was drained of all his rage; he only felt the curiosity of hunger, pitiful and greedy. All his attention was now concentrated on the piece of bread that Serag chewed without interest, his eyes half closed with sleep. It was as if the child had discovered some marvelous world. He advanced a few steps, hypnotized by the piece of bread, and stopped in the middle of the path, his legs spread, his mouth open, trembling under his rags.

A huge cloud detached itself, exposing the discolored sun. All the countryside was bathed in a humid, cold light which created enormous distances, as if the earth had suddenly withdrawn its horizons. Serag trembled, blinked his eyes; the light of day bothered him and irritated his nerves. He had noticed the child's gaze, but pretended not to see him, and continued to eat his bread in the resigned attitude of one condemned to death. At each moment he felt sleep reach out inexorably for him. He let himself fall back, leaned on his elbows and finally abandoned himself to sleep. He felt no more fear; he simply wished to go to sleep. He closed his eyes and lay like a shipwreck on the wet grass and fell asleep.

This only lasted a second. He quickly regained consciousness, sensing the child's presence and the fierce demand of his stare. Brusquely he decided to get up and leave; this halt had only succeeded in making him more lethargic. As usual, he was roaming in this vicinity to observe the factory under construction. The factory was still several hundred meters further on, isolated in the open country. Serag no longer desired to go there; he was tired from all these emotions and found himself more feeble and discouraged than ever. He hesitated, thinking of returning to the house, when the child moved and manifested his presence by a plaintive groan. There was no longer a way to avoid him.

"Hello, little one!"

Serag had called out without thinking, as if to give himself a hold on a vague and depressing reality. The child came running, crossed the path with a few rapid leaps, his rags fluttering like wings. Serag saw him suddenly before him, miserable and pale, holding his slingshot in one hand, the other hand empty, impatient.

"Do you want a piece?"

The child held out his hand without answering. He seemed defiant, his incredible eyes fixed on Serag. No doubt he had long ago lost all trust and was waiting for some frightful trap. Serag broke the bread and gave him the biggest piece.

"You've been hunting a long time?"

The child's mouth was already full. He replied, as if he wanted to get away:

"Yes, for a long time. What of it?"

Serag now saw him from too near not to be struck by his jaundiced color, his scowl, his air of deep craftiness. He had big loose ears, and his shaven head was covered with running sores. A scar cut across the corner of his upper lip, contorting his face in a horrible smirk. Under his rags one could see his slender body and supple limbs, scaly with the dirt of the roads. This was truly a terrible being, come from a world of combat and despair. Now Serag understood the anguish that he created around him. It was not simply due to his misery, nor to his expression of a precocious criminal. No, this anguish was the message of a hostile and troubled universe, lost, ages before, of which he was only the pale and unconscious reflection. He gave the impression of a pitiful trapped animal, destined for the worst fate, and constantly the victim of latent dangers. What dangers? This was just what Serag had wanted to learn: the obscure mystery which enveloped the hard life of men.

The child devoured his bread with feverish haste. He still wasn't sure about this providential meal.

"Well, do you like to hunt birds?" Serag asked.

The child stopped eating. He seemed to be gravely offended.

"I don't do it for fun," he said. "I hunt them so I can sell them. Do you think I've got time to waste?"

He assumed an air of importance, looking almost with pity at Serag.

"Excuse me. I didn't know you were working. It's nice work you have there."

"It's damned hard work," replied the child. "Since this morning I haven't killed a single one. They're worse than devils."

To sell birds! Certainly it was a business as worthy as any other. Serag realized this perfectly. But even so, it seemed a little fantastic to him, a little too frivolous. Was the child making fun of him? He must scorn him. Yet he remembered the child's cruel efforts and couldn't help marveling at him. Perhaps this was the sort of work for him. He would have liked to ask for explanations, to know the details of this mad industry, rich in risks and adventures. Perhaps, one day, he himself could take up this work, if he judged it sufficiently lucrative.

"And this brings you a lot of money?" he asked.

The child didn't reply. He had finished eating his bread, but seemed scarcely appeased. Suddenly he began to jump on one leg, spinning around like a maniac. This exercise plunged him into a state of rare intoxication. His face had taken on an expression of careless joy. He scarcely paid any more attention to Serag and seemed to have forgotten him completely.

Stretched out on the grass, Serag watched the child turn; then he blinked his eyes to keep himself from dizziness. He was shocked by the child's contradictory behavior and understood nothing of his changes of mood. His imagination reveled in a savage reality which only included the child intermittently. He swung between an absurd dream and a terrifying reality. Serag couldn't manage to place him in any part of his pathetic image of a world tortured by agony.

A fine rain began to fall, making the country still more melancholy. Serag was aroused from his torpor by the drops of rain striking his face. He sat up, shook himself, and remained sitting on the grass, his arms clasped around his knees. After a minute the rain stopped and a vague light shone down. The sun emerged from the clouds, then again was caught by the heavy mass of phantom ships.

The child still spun around; he was panting—at the height of ecstasy. Serag noticed that the leg he held in the air was wrapped in an old piece of cloth, just above the heel.

"Did you hurt your foot?"

"I was run over by a streetcar," replied the child, and he stopped turning.

"It's better now?"

"Yes, it's better. But it's not important. Tell me: haven't you any more bread?"

"No," said Serag, "I only had the piece we ate. I'm very sorry. Are you still hungry?"

"I'm always hungry," said the child. "And you, what are you going to do afterwards?"

"After what? What do you mean?"

"I mean when you're hungry again," explained the child.

"Why I'll go back to the house for lunch," said Serag.

"Ah! you're one of the ones who have houses!"

"Yes," said Serag innocently. "I have a house not far from here, near the highway."

But at once he was ashamed and saw that the child was judging him with deep suspicion.

"You see," he continued, "it's not really my house, it's my father's. I only live there. And you, haven't you a house?"

"I had one," said the child. "But someone stole it."

"Someone stole it? How? Who stole it from you?"

"A boy I rented half of it to. We shared it together. But one night when I came back to sleep, I couldn't find the boy or the box."

"The box?" said Serag, astonished. "What box?"

"The house—it was a wooden box," said the child. "You didn't think I owned a real house did you?"

"I just didn't understand," Serag apologized.

"Anyhow, it was a beautiful box," said the child regretfully. "I found it near a junkyard. It kept out the cold very well, especially where I set it up. It was better than an apartment, believe me. We had some good times, that boy and me. It was warm there and we smoked butts. Sometimes some of our friends would come by and keep us company."

"You all lived inside? It must have been a big box."

"No, the others stayed outside. Only the boy and me lived in the box. It was ours."

"And you never invited them to stay with you?"

"Sometimes one of them would take my place for a minute. But he wouldn't stay long. We threw him out if he didn't want to go."

"Then this boy stole it from you?"

"Yes, he was a thief and a son of a bitch. I spend my time looking for him. Have you seen him around here?"

"No, I haven't seen him. Besides, how would I recognize him?"

"Oh! he's easy to recognize," said the child. "His mother's the biggest whore in the world."

This story left Serag dreaming for a moment. He imagined the child's adventurous existence with secret joy. To be like him! It wasn't only the adventure that seduced him, but the vague conviction that beyond this unfettered and nomadic existence was a living and tangible reality he wanted to share. For a long time he had fought to free himself from the apathy that was like an open wound, draining the very blood of his youth. He would have liked to feel overwhelming emotions, to face horrible dangers, to fight with the endurance of a living being. But at the same time he was vaguely frightened by this unknown universe, cursed and suffering. Dark forebodings warned him not to attempt such a trying ordeal. The feeling of his impotence crushed him, always threw him back toward the world of idleness where he vegetated in his family's house, surrounded by a security more annihilating than death. Never had he dreamed of this liberty of action, this pitiless intensity for life which the child exuded. He had the impression that between himself and the world of this child there was an infinite desert of black slumber.

The birds had come back to the branches of the sycamore. They seemed happy with their lot and filled the air with sharp calls. From time to time the child glared toward them; he didn't forgive them for their deception and thought of soon resuming his interrupted work. It was a ruined day for him—again one of those endless days when he searched in vain for his subsistence. But he seemed not to worry, shivering under his rags with a sort of naive aliveness, as if all his woes had no effect on his hardened nature. He crossed his arms on his chest and began to jump joyously.

Serag stretched weakly, tried to get up, and fell back at once on the grass. He made a second effort and succeeded this time in standing up. He blinked his eyes and spoke to the child:

"Let's walk a bit, little one! I ought to go as far as the factory. Would you like to come with me?"

"Is there a factory near here?"

"Yes, it's still under construction. I don't know what's wrong, but for months they've stopped work there."

"Maybe the owner is dead," said the child.

"I don't think so," said Serag. Then he added in a lugubrious tone: "That would be a great tragedy!"

"Why, is he a relative of yours?"

"No, it's not that. But I'm interested in the factory. If you'll go with me I'll explain it to you."

He felt painfully the need of company. At bottom, he knew he'd never get as far as the factory alone—that he'd surely fall asleep on the way. This had already happened to him several times.

"I can't come with you," said the child. "I have to go on hunting." He hesitated a moment. "But if you'll give me a half piastre, I'll come. I haven't a house to eat in. You understand!"

Serag fumbled in his pockets, drew out a collection of junk, among which was a two milliemes piece. It was a souvenir he had kept for a long time. Suddenly he had remembered it.

"I haven't much money with me right now," he said to the child, holding the coin out to him, "but here are two milliemes. Will that do?"

"We won't haggle,' said the child. "It's all right, let's go!"

II

The path they followed was hidden by the corn field. The child walked ahead—limping, either because of his injured foot, or only to give himself the air of an heroic martyr. Ever since he had touched his two coins he had abandoned himself, overflowing with unbelievable energy. He had torn off an ear of corn, crunched the hard kernels, then spat them on the ground with disgust. Serag paid no attention to him. He felt only his presence, and his gesticulating walk kept him from sleep. He moved forward like a sleepwalker, his brain invaded by thick clouds.

For a moment the cold became very sharp. Serag shivered at each blast of wind. His red woollen sweater, with its rolled up collar, scarcely protected him. But this seemed only a minor evil. He was really oppressed by his shoes. As always, when he went out to look at the factory, he wore his old football shoes, a survival from his years at school, and they weighted down his steps and bruised his feet. No mere whim governed his choice of this strange gear; it had a profound meaning for him. Serag wished to prove to himself, in venturing on this pilgrimage, that he was making a dangerous expedition. The idea of performing some daring feat filled him with a certain fervor. Without this fervor he wouldn't have had the courage to try anything. Therefore, he suffered the football shoes, as a torment necessary to his liberation.

Suddenly the path grew wider, and they found themselves in the middle of a field planted in clover. A peasant's hut of dried mud, partly in ruins, stood on the edge of an ancient trench filled with weeds. Nearby, a dismantled sakieh lay in the dust. Serag stopped; he could go no farther. He stumbled down the side of a furrow and dissolved in tears.

The child continued on alone for several steps, then turned and came back toward Serag.

"You paid me to come with you. Let's keep going."

"I'm tired," implored Serag. "Have pity on me."

"You're crying," the child observed, puzzled. "Why? Are you sick?"

"It's nothing. I'm not sick. I'm just tired. Give me one more minute."

"I can't wait," said the child. "Stop crying. What a day this is! There probably isn't any factory at all."

"There is a factory," said Serag. "On my honor, you'll see it soon. We aren't very far now."

"Why do you want to go there?"

"I'll explain in a little while. You'll see. It's very interesting."

The child pondered a long time. What drew this sleepy young man to see a factory? After puzzling awhile he seemed to have found out.

"Tell me: you're not looking for treasure by any chance?"

"No, it isn't treasure," said Serag. "It's only a factory under construction. Believe me, there isn't any treasure."

"It doesn't matter," said the child. "Maybe we can find some treasure anyway. Now get up! I've waited long enough. This day's wasted for me."

Serag got up painfully, ran his fingers through his hair, then searched the horizon as if trying to orient himself. A pile of twigs burned somewhere behind the high stalks of corn. In the distance, some crows fled under the low clouds. Serag recognized the place, put his hand on the child's shoulder and prepared to take up his march again.

They didn't walk long. Coming to the end of the field, they turned left, crossed a dry pond, then climbed a little hillock.

"Here's the factory," said Serag.

In a large stretch of land, lying fallow like wild country, the unfinished factory lay in the middle of a mass of rubbish and crumbling scaffolds. It was a strange and awful place, uneven with quagmires, forbidding. It seemed more like a wrecking yard. There were only the fronts of walls, half constructed— a whole derelict architecture partially completed, abandoned to the briars. All around fragments of old iron and rough stone were lying in the dirt. In a corner at the far end of the field were piles of corrugated iron, covered with a heavy layer of rust. Work seemed to have been stopped a long time; it was already more than six months since Serag had seen anyone there. He couldn't understand the reason for this. Two or three times a week he came here to take a look, in the hope of seeing the masons resume their work. But it was always the same deception. The factory remained as it was, giving the impression of a phantom or a stage set.

The child had lost his mocking exuberance. He seemed dismayed, in the grip of some pitiful fear. It was apparent that he'd forgotten the treasure.

"Is that the factory?" he asked.

"Yes," replied Serag. "I wonder why they don't finish it. I'd like to work there."

"What kind of factory is it?"

"I think it's for textiles. I want to apply for a job."

"And if they don't finish it?"

"Then I'll never be able to work," said Serag wearily.

"Why, are you out of work now?"

"Well, you see, I've never worked yet. But I'm very anxious to begin."

"You're crazy," said the child. "You want to work in a factory! What a day for your mother!"

"Listen, little one! I want to work; I think I'll be able to do a lot of things."

"What can you do?"

"I don't know yet. But a man has to work, don't you think?"

"You've got a house where you can eat and you want to work! What a joke."

They stood for a few minutes without speaking.

"Why don't you look for a job in the city if you want to work so much?" the child began. "Because if you ask me, this factory would make a good latrine."

"I can't go to the city," said Serag. "It's too far. The good thing about this factory, you see, is that it's so close to our house. I won't get too tired coming here."

"You get tired very fast. Are you sick?"

Serag didn't answer. The nearness of the factory was an excuse he clung to in despair. In his heart, he knew the factory would never be finished and, because of this, he would never run any risk of working there. When he faced this deceit, Serag despised himself. He was unhappy and made endless reproaches to himself. Then, to justify himself, he would say it was only a beginning but that what he had already done was a satisfactory start. The courage it had taken to make this pilgrimage, to look at the place where he ought to have worked, was already enough to merit esteem and confidence. He gave a last look at the unfinished factory, fortified himself with the idea that he was already on the road of social progress, and congratulated himself inwardly.

The sky continued to drift its malevolent clouds into remnants. A heartbreaking and secret melancholy crept into the folds of the landscape, invading the country like the approach of evening. Near the unfinished factory, a starving dog wandered among the rubbish. It sniffed everywhere, without insistence, as if it had already lost all hope, then vanished behind a wall. Serag waited to see it reappear, then turned towards the child. He was behaving wildly again, shooting in the air with his slingshot, without concern for a target, simply for the pleasure of moving. He seemed no longer interested in Serag; and he had returned to his vagabonding life. Suddenly he stopped and asked, as if disturbed:

"What time is it?"

Serag started, looking at him without understanding.

'The time?" he said. "I don't know. I haven't a watch. Are you in a hurry?"

"All rich people have watches," said the child sententiously. "There are lots of rich people in the city. They even have gold watches; I've seen them."

"Some day, I hope, you'll have a gold watch too," said Serag.

"Me!" cried the child. "It's impossible. Unless I steal it."

"Ah well! you'll steal it."

On the road back, the child closed himself in morose silence. He no longer limped, having assumed an air of abused dignity. Decidedly, he understood there was no more to be gained from his chance companion. He was ready to leave him at once. Other adventures called him.

Coming to the highway, they stopped. Serag drew his hands from his pockets, stood a moment, his arms swinging, not knowing how to separate from the child. He remembered he hadn't yet learned his name.

"What's your name?" he asked.

"Antar," the child replied.

He had flung his name like a defiance.

Serag was disappointed; the name Antar seemed wrong, too pretentious for the memory he wished to keep of the child. He asked again:

'Tell me, haven't you another name?"

"Another name!" the child was astonished. "Why? Don't you like this one?"

Serag was embarrassed and couldn't explain himself.

"I'd like to know if you haven't another name; that is, a nicer one—a nickname. For instance, the name your mother calls you when she plays with you."

"By Allah! You're a fool!" cried the child. "Do I look like a drooling baby to be played with?"

"Don't be angry. I didn't mean to insinuate anything. If you ever come back this way, don't forget to come see me. My name is Serag," he shouted after the retreating child.

The child left, and suddenly Serag found himself terribly alone. He stayed by the side of the road a few minutes, undecided, then started to walk towards the house.

It was a large asphalt road, bordered by old trees. Serag walked in the middle of it, his back stooped and his eyes fixed on the ground, sifting the disturbing details of his meeting with the child. He was gone now, with his strange ardor and his passion for life. Since he had left, Serag felt an emptiness he had never experienced before. A car raced by a few inches from him, its muffler open. An odor of exhaust fumes spread in the air, stung his nostrils and almost suffocated him. He coughed; his eyes brimmed with tears. He went over to the side of the road, waited a moment until the cough stopped, then tranquilly began to walk on. Again the memory of the child came to him, and he thought of abandoning everything to rejoin him. He stopped, looked behind in hopes that perhaps he'd see him again, but the highway was empty as far as the horizon.

From time to time he would pass a villa, surrounded by an iron grill and with its shutters closed. A whole world at its ease lived there in permanence, sickly and proud in its retirement. Serag wondered what they could be plotting behind those walls— those people buried in their miserable lives like rats at the bottom of their holes. What absurd degradation! And all around him the same thing. Wouldn't he ever get out of this enormous farce, this stagnation? Surely there must be some part of the world where there were living beings and not these pitiful corpses. But where?

On his right there was now a large block of houses, a few of three and four stories, unpretentious and some very old, with falling plaster. Here lived the petty bourgeois—retired civil servants—who had fled the uproar of the city to come and grow mouldy on the hideous outskirts of this street. Farther along, the houses had invaded the fields on both sides of the road and spread like a city across the tillage. Narrow alleys were formed between them; alleys of packed earth on the uneven, rubbish covered ground. Linen of all colors was drying in the windows, the only bright spots that cheered the desolate, grey agglomeration, a little. A few people made fugitive appearances, as if to give death one rude contradiction.

Serag turned toward the right side of the road. For a distance of ten yards some low one-story constructions stood in a line. They were a group of shops devoted to small trade. Serag stopped in front of the first shop.

"Greetings, Abou Zeid."

The man squatting on the steps of his shop raised his head, became somehow animated without stirring, and replied to the young man with a resigned carelessness. He was singularly filthy, with bloodshot eyes and a toothless, slobbering mouth. A shaggy beard, badly dyed, ravaged this face of a somnolent prophet. He wore a skullcap of braided linen, and a long brown shawl covered most of his body. Peacefully leaning against a wall of the shop, he warmed himself in the scant rays of a hesitant and colorless sun. Some baskets filled with peanuts, a few withered peas, and some watermelon seeds were near him on a low shelf. Inside, the shop was empty.

"How's business?" asked Serag.

"Allah curse business and those who invented it!" replied Abou Zeid. "It's an evil sent for my old age. I just manage to eke out the rent of this cursed store."

"It's a big shire for selling peanuts, Abou Zeid, my father! I've already told you. Besides, selling peanuts isn't a trade for a man."

"What's a man to do, my son?" murmured Abou Zeid, "You haven't yet bit upon an idea? I'm in your hands."

"I'm still looking," said Serag.

He went up to one of the baskets, took a handful of withered nuts and put them greedily in his mouth. He chewed them a long time, perplexed, troubled by a strange uneasiness. Actually, he didn't know what role to play before this ridiculous shop. It wasn't the sort of work he wanted to be near; it was only one of the malicious aspects of a public laziness. Abou Zeid leveled a look of atonement at him, full of resolute stupidity and shrewd admiration. For a long time he had complained to the young man that his shop was too large to sell peanuts. He felt an instinctive sympathy for him, in whom curiosity and the passion for sleep mixed. As for Serag, he often came to gossip with the old vendor; above all he loved to hear the obscene stories of his many conjugal crises. Abou Zeid knew the reputation of the young man's relatives and held their eccentricities in high esteem, finding them to his own taste. He was strongly inclined to a certain form of chronic torpor himself. Thus a business suggestion coming from a family so idle could in no way be dangerous nor, above all, threaten much work. Abou Zeid waited, peace in his soul, for the young man to squander his generous advice.

There was a moment of silence. From time to time, Abou Zeid scratched under his clothing, caught a louse and crushed it between his nails, closing his eyes with satisfaction. He seemed to be performing a solemn ritual, moving with a calculated slowness. After having exterminated some of these undesirables, he asked suddenly, his face almost jovial:

"Tell me, my son, is it true that your brother Galal bids you all goodbye before going to bed?"

"Why should he say goodbye? Please talk sense."

"It seems he sleeps for a whole month without waking," continued Abou Zeid. "Is that true, my son?"

A smile of admiration touched his toothless mouth like a wound.

"It's malicious gossip," said Serag. "How could you believe such things? It's true my brother Galal sleeps a great deal. Sometimes a whole day. But to sleep for a month—no one in the world could do it. Believe me, it's nothing but gossip."

"The world is so spiteful," said Abou Zeid with a certain deceit. "Men say so many things."

Serag was deeply humiliated. He remembered having already heard such stories about his brother. It was true that Galal had broken all records for sleep and was even capable of worse performances. He only woke to eat or to go to the bathroom. But from this to accuse him of sleeping for a whole month, surely it was an exaggeration. Serag wondered if the public included him in this vice. He suffered under the weight of inertia that bound him to his family. His youth still saved him, but how much longer? Work was the only thing that could rescue him, but it was such a remote possibility, he didn't dare think of it.

Next door, in the tinker's shop, a workman twisted over an unwieldy pot while a small boy helped him work the ancient bellows of the forge. Some winter flies moved about silently, but persistently. Abou Zeid drove them away with a controlled and cunning gesture of his hand. At another shop a servant who was doing his marketing swore heatedly at a vegetable seller who had allowed himself to make a joke. His voice echoed in the middle of the road like that of a hysterical madman, as though someone had tried to violate him or tear out his eyes. Abou Zeid tossed his head at this show of human depravity, then took up the train of his mediocre thoughts again. He had just found an idea for his business that seemed congenial.

"About the shop, my son, what do you think of my selling radishes? They're beautiful—radishes!"

"It's not bad," acknowledged Serag. "But it's still not right. Just the same—think of filling this shop with radishes. It would be amusing."

"What's really amusing," said Abou Zeid, "is to see it empty as it is right now. Believe me, it gives me a scare."

"Be patient a few more days. I promised to put my mind to it. You know, Abou Zeid, at the moment I've a few worries myself. When things are going better, I'll find a really spectacular idea for your business."

"Allah watch over you, my son! Only you'd do well to hurry. And above all, try not to bring me ideas that are original and tiring. I'm an old man; I can't allow myself to have fancies. As you see, my strength declines day by day. But I have confidence in you. May God help you!"

Abou Zeid's laments originated in a conjugal drama which he had never mentioned to the young man. His pride had kept him silent. Abou Zeid was the victim of a nagging mother in law's ambition. She kept after him all day, calling him a misshapen monster, unfit, and a failure at business. She made his life unbearable and incited her daughter to rebel. Abou Zeid was reduced by this to beg caresses from his wife. To escape the reproaches of this fury, he had, several months before, quit the little corner of the street where he had sold his merchandise in order to rent this shop. Here he had consecrated himself to becoming a famous tradesman. He now found himself in a trap and was trying to avoid, as much as possible, the disaster that menaced him.

A bus passed, stopping at a nearby station. Some men got out and walked without haste toward their homes. No doubt they were coming back from work, but from what sort of work? Serag observed them with a certain contempt. They didn't seem harassed, but rather sad. They must have been sleeping in their dusty offices at the bottom of some corporation. The thing that annoyed them above all, was that they couldn't sleep in their own homes. They had to disturb themselves and go elsewhere to sleep, in order to give the impression they were doing important work. Serag thought them contemptible. They walked off and the bus went on its way, spitting out a great jet of blue smoke.

With the corner of his shawl, Abou Zeid wiped the saliva that was soiling his beard; then he straightened his baskets a little and asked with much interest:

"Why are you worried, my son? Is it—I pray not—that you're sick?"

"I'm not sick," replied Serag. "I'm very well. Goodbye."

Why were they all asking if he were sick? The child too had asked. Did they see something in his face? He walked on a moment, then turned to the right and entered a little alley of hard dirt. After a few feet, he stopped before the iron railing of his house. It was a small villa, shabby in appearance, two stories high. A tiny garden, rapidly filling with rubbish, separated it from the alley. Setag had stopped, his back turned to the villa. He didn't dare go back into the house; he feared the moment of finding himself with his family again. The sun had come out; entirely free of the clouds, it gave out a penetrating heat. Serag felt warm again, forgot his torments and sank back in an endless revery.

III

Standing in front of the kitchen sink, Hoda was washing a dish. Her tongue between her teeth, her elbows resting on the edge of the sink, she hurried with the precise movements of the well trained domestic. Through the window came the strong rays of the sun, spotting the flags of the floor with dazzling splashes of light. The kitchen was the only clean place in the house, it was her domain, and no one ever penetrated it. Hoda could clean there at her leisure without the usual trials. In the other rooms, cleaning was a hazardous affair that required much patience and discretion. The family was always on the verge of falling asleep and didn't like to have her working around. Hoda had learned all sorts of devices for putting at least a semblance of order in the house.

In spite of the deafening noise of the oil stove, she heard from the dining room the sound of Rafik's piercing voice, impatient with the company of Uncle Mustapha. Hoda stopped a moment and listened. She was afraid it was because of her again. It was always the same story: she was late with lunch. Actually, it wasn't her fault; the habits of the house kept her from coming earlier in the morning. For one thing, Galal had expressly forbidden it. Although she always managed to get in without being seen, the mere knowledge that someone was awake in the house kept him from sleeping. He would have preferred never to have her there at all. He complained about the slightest disturbance around him. His sensitivity was miraculous. He seemed to be equipped with antennae that warned him of the least change in the atmosphere. He was the easiest to satisfy in this strange family, but became intransigent as soon as something concerned his sleep. His complaints were weak, unsuccessful stirrings in the abyss. Even the caresses he allowed himself with her were always almost innocuous, discouraged, and terribly monotonous. Because of this, Hoda wasn't much afraid of him. She always managed to escape his summary embrace without great damage.

She stood on tiptoe, reached the faucet and turned it on full force. Then she passed some soap covered plates under the stream of water. Soon they were clean and shining. Hoda admired them complacently for it gave her a childish joy to see these immaculate things come from her hands. It was one of the rare satisfactions in her wretched life. But suddenly a thought darkened her face. She had just remembered she hadn't seen Serag this morning. She had hunted in vain for him in his room. She wondered where he could be. Undoubtedly, he had gone out early. He was the only one in this sleep-besieged house who behaved a little as though he were alive. Hoda was glad he was not like the others; yet she feared all sorts of dangers for him. One never knew what could happen to a boy like him, left all alone to the hazards of the streets, among evil people and things. She saw him crushed by a car, or asleep, in a field, helpless against the sting of a scorpion. She stood for a moment speculative and uneasy, her tongue still between her teeth, the last dish in her dripping hands.

She caught herself, and thought with dismay of the late lunch. And to complete her anxiety, the lentils weren't done. Hoda left the sink, raised the cover of the pot on the stove and dipped the soup ladle into the steaming lentils, tasting them with the end of her tongue. They were cooked, but not salted enough. Hoda took a handful of salt from a jar, threw it in the pot and put the cover back on.

Now she must find Serag and tell him lunch was ready; then wake Galal who was sleeping, as always, with his head buried under his quilt. Old Hafez ate alone in his room on the top floor. He was never disturbed, living in almost complete isolation. Hoda had been ordered by him to bring his meals to his room. She was responsible for everything and took care of the family as if it consisted of sick children.

She wiped the plates, stacking them in a pile to carry to the dining room. At this instant, as she turned her head toward the window, she saw Serag standing in the alley, his back turned toward the house. Her heart trembled. Instinctively, she wanted to call to him, but found herself unable to pronounce a word, held back by his strange pose. Serag was standing very erect, his hands thrust in his pockets, his head thrown back, his face held up to the sun. He seemed to be contemplating something fascinating in the sky. Hoda couldn't see his face, and that intrigued her even more. What could he be gazing at, motionless as a statue? Hoda put the stack of plates on the table and crept to the window.

Serag was still in his ecstasy, cut off, entirely lost in some dream. Hoda raised her head, looked at the house opposite, then at the sky where light clouds were scattering in the wind. There was nothing unusual to hold the attention. No doubt, Serag wasn't looking at anything. Perhaps his eyes were even closed. What a strange boy! He could stay that way forever. Hoda stood still for a long time, hoping to see him move, then decided to open the window.

"Serag! Lunch is ready!"

Several seconds went by before the young man turned his head. Seeing Hoda, he made a face of annoyance, then smiled sadly. Hoda saw him open the gate to the garden. She ran to pick up the pile of dishes and started toward the dining room.

"Well, you bitch, is lunch ready?' asked Rafik.

"It's ready," said Hoda. "You can sit down at the table."

"Hurry up, you daughter of a whore!"

The dining room, on the first floor, was large, with black and white tiling, furnished with a few moth-eaten chairs. Except for the table and chairs, there was only a buffet and a couch, covered by a white cloth with yellow stripes, repulsively dirty. A rather large mat of braided straw covered the tiles under the table. The walls were bare and sweating from the humidity. Like all the rooms in the house, the dining room gave off a special odor of mustiness—the stale air of closed houses, of a vault or a cavern. On one of the walls, in a gold frame, was a huge photograph of old Hafez, retouched with water colors. Because of the dust and flyspecks that had completely covered the glass, old Hafez looked like a horrible daubed corpse. Old Hafez, who never left his room, found this a means of presiding, in a rather terrifying manner, at his children's meals. But no one paid any attention to him; he grew dimmer in his gold frame, gradually forgotten in the general indifference.

Rafik was stretched out on the couch, dressed in dirty pajamas, his feet bare except for wooden shoes. He had just finished a very animated conversation with Uncle Mustapha, during which he had riddled him with sarcasms. Now he was relaxed, taking malicious pleasure in his uncle's crestfallen face. Uncle Mustapha was already at the table, silently at his place, nibbling a piece of bread while he waited for lunch. He had assumed an imperturbable calm, even though he was deeply shaken. Rafik's sarcasm always wounded his dignity, and he tried to compose himself in an attitude of serenity, which, unfortunately, fooled no one.

Hoda arranged the plates on the table and started back toward the kitchen. Rafik had been watching her malevolently. As she passed him, he grabbed her by a corner of her dress and asked in a low voice:

"Tell me: have you seen her?"

"Yes, I saw her," replied Hoda.

Rank had a gleam like hope in his eye. His voice became deeper, agonized.

"What did she say?"

"She said she didn't want to see you."

"Bitch! You're lying!"

Hoda tried to free herself, but Rafik held on to her dress. She feared him more than all the others, because of this gleam of lust always burning in his eyes. He seemed possessed by a constant fury.

"It's not my fault," she defended herself. "I can't do anything about it. She told me she didn't want to see you."

"It's impossible," said Rafik. "It's impossible she's forgotten me."

"She hasn't forgotten you," said Hoda. "She just doesn't want to see you."

"The whore! And you, you're another!"

"Let go of me," begged Hoda.

Rafik released her and fell back on the sofa. Hoda went back to the kitchen.

During this hushed dialogue, Uncle Mustapha gaped, his eyes fixed on some invisible point in the room. The bitterness of his thoughts led him inevitably to one of his prolonged withdrawals that astonished the household. He seemed to be always vegetating in some other world. He wandered about all day in his nightgown and an old jacket of maroon wool, his tarboosh always on his head for fear of the cold. In this garb Uncle Mustapha gave the impression of being there only for a visit. His endless displays of dignity tired him enormously. To maintain his self-respect among these lazy and disrespectful children was a job he found more and more exhausting. Uncle Mustapha took much pain to safeguard, in his present situation, a remnant of this solemn dignity which had been his prerogative long ago. From time to time during several minutes, he emitted strange sighs that seemed to come from some deep-rooted suffering.

"Here's our great labourer!" said Rafik suddenly.

Serag had just come into the dining room. He had taken off his football shoes in his bedroom and now was walking around in his socks, with an uncertain step, his face tired as though he hadn't slept for many days. Slowly he took his place at the table. His morning walk had left him rather exhausted and he was glad to find himself back with his family. Each time he came back from a hike across the countryside, he felt as though he had escaped some sinister danger. Then the desire to wander seized him again, and he began to hate this atmosphere of mystery and sleep that smothered him. At this moment he was smiling, almost contentedly.

"Hello, Uncle," he said.

"Hello, my son."

"Well," said Rafik, "what good news do you bring from the outside?"

"I didn't see much," replied Serag. "I just walked in the country."

"Not really! You look so tired. And where do you think you'll drag yourself next?"

"That's none of your business," said Serag. "I'm free to walk where I want."

"You walk!" sneered Rafik. "Look where you're walking now. I think you were looking for work. But excuse me, I see you've given up that folly."

"Go to hell!" said Serag.

"Leave the boy alone," said Uncle Mustapha.

"Uncle Mustapha," replied Rafik, "you've lived in the city a long time; tell us, please, what men who work do."

"I don't know what you're talking about," said his uncle. "What are you trying to say?"

"It's a question that only concerns Serag," insisted Rafik. "He'll have to prove himself. I can hardly wait till he brings some money back to the house. Because my dear Serag, I hope that with all your talents you'll earn a lot of money."

Serag was used to this insulting irony and didn't answer. Only Uncle Mustapha always rose to his nephew's bait. He couldn't resist, even though he had been around him for almost three years. His bewilderment at such moments was pitiably funny. Rafik found him the perfect target and never lost an opportunity to abuse him. Actually, it wasn't that he was innately malicious; he simply needed a release to calm his nerves which were continually on edge. Rafik's sarcasm covered a painful sorrow; for at bottom he was the only sane person in his whole family. He had consciously chosen the quiet destiny that bound the native idleness of a whole clan. His reason, as well as his own temperament, had drawn him to it. He could analyze everything that such a destiny of disinterested grandeur meant and was provoked to see others not seemingly aware of their good fortune. From this came his scorn and sarcasm.

Since his conversation with Hoda, his face betrayed a strong annoyance that he tried to control but which shone through each of his words. He got up from the couch and took his place opposite Uncle Mustapha.

Hoda came back from the kitchen with the pot of lentils and placed them in the middle of the table.

"Help yourselves," she said. "I have to wake Galal."

"Have you served the bey?" asked Uncle Mustapha.

"The bey!" Rafik exclaimed. "What a sense of humour! Since when, Uncle Mustapha, is my father a bey?"

Uncle Mustapha reflected but didn't answer. He wanted to find some ingenious formula to safeguard his dignity.

"Your father's a bey," he said. "And I too am a bey. If you weren't so disrespectful, that's what you'd call me. You above all, Rafik. You forget I was a rich man."

"I haven't forgotten a thing," said Rafik. "Uncle Mustapha, you're really quite a man. You should have been a minister of state."

Uncle Mustapha sensed his helplessness and held back his irritation. He began to serve himself some lentils, then said with a detached air:

"You're only a bad boy. Anyhow, I'm not going to talk to you anymore."

"Oh, this is terrible. You're not going to talk to me anymore! What'll I do? Uncle Mustapha, answer me; it isn't true—you're not angry with me?"

Rafik put on a tragic face and fixed imploring eyes on Uncle Mustapha. But Uncle Mustapha didn't budge. He kept silent and began to eat tranquilly, absentmindedly. Serag helped himself too; he was eating hungrily. The visit to the factory had made him ravenous. The suffering he felt outside was gone; he appreciated this peaceful security where there were no catastrophes. Rafik's harangues with Uncle Mustapha created an atmosphere of complicity around him, a familiar warmth that enchanted him.

Silence reigned everywhere in the room. No one spoke. In the middle of the table the pot of lentils gave off steam that rose toward the ceiling in vaporous white clouds. Old Hafez, gloomy and smeared, disappeared little by little under the mist that filmed the glass of the picture. Finally, he disappeared altogether.

"Why are you awake?"

Galal, who had just asked this anguished question, was standing in the doorway with the frightened look of someone who has just awakened with a start. His eyes were still half closed; he yawned till he twisted his jaw. His disheveled hair fell on his forehead, and his face had a cadaverous pallor. He wore a large nightgown; foully dirty and stained with sweat, it clung to his skin. Obviously, he hadn't changed it for months. Leaning against the wall, he stood without moving, blinking his eyes swollen with sleep, as if he wanted to take in everything in the scene.

"If we're awake, my dear Galal, it's only to eat," said Rafik. "I swear it on my honor. Don't think anything else."

"I thought there must have been a fire!" said Galal with a gasp.

He came forward unsteadily and slipped into a free place at the table. He waited a moment, to take up consciousness again, to realize fully his state of being awake. He seemed very unhappy to be in action and obliged to move. His timid manners and mechanical gestures were like acts of daring revived each day. He served himself, sniffed his plate before putting it down in front of him and became motionless again. He still felt the remains of sleep—of a particular savor—and he wanted to make it last as long as possible. But soon he began to eat.

"Tell me, are the lentils good?" he asked.

"They're rotten," replied Rafik. "What else do you expect from this girl?"

"This is no life," said Galal. "All day long we're upset by worries."

"You're wrong to be bothered," said Rafik. "You could easily give up eating. Try it, you'll see it's not so bad."

"I'll try," said Galal, "when you're all dead."

"O shame!" cried Uncle Mustapha. "Is that how you insult your father?"

"Who insulted my father?" asked Galal, disturbed.

"You just said, a second ago, 'when you're all dead.' You Galal, you, the oldest—you're a bad example to your brothers."

Galal began to eat, indifferent to his uncle's reproaches. Everything that happened around him was only illusion, vile conspiracies against the splendid web of sleep. He lived in the midst of his family completely immune to its quibbling. They were after him all the time with their little intrigues, but he always knew how to escape. Actually they were only weak novices who knew nothing of the delights of this drug like oblivion. Galal was several years ahead of them. Uncle Mustapha was still the most obtuse. He had only been living in the house for three years. What could he understand? When he was living alone in the city, he must have spent his time seeing people, going out every night, enjoying the company of easy women—an intemperate existence, without repose. At first, he used to come often to gossip with Galal. What did he take him for? Galal slept on and didn't answer. It took Uncle Mustapha a long time to understand. Now, he didn't disturb Galal except on grave occasions.

Hoda came back from the kitchen and sat down at the table near Serag. She always ate with the family. She was the daughter of one of old Hafez's distant relatives, a miserable widow who had no one but her in the world. Old Hafez had hired her for practically nothing. She came every day to clean the house, fix the meals, and then returned in the evening to her mother, who lived in the neighborhood. She was considered as a member of the family, and not as a servant.

"Have you taken lunch up to the bey?" asked Uncle Mustapha.

"Yes," said Hoda. "I just did."

"Uncle Mustapha," said Rafik, "if you keep calling my father bey, I'm going to lose my temper and do something you won't like."

"But why, my son?"

"Because I don't like privilege."

"What insolence!" said Uncle Mustapha. "And besides, I'm not talking to you."

"All the more," Rafik continued, "since the bey in question is getting ready to be married. On my honor, that's going to be a beautiful wedding!"

"Be quiet!" said Uncle Mustapha. "That's none of your business. By Allah! Have you ever seen such an insolent boy?"

"That's why you've been calling him bey lately! You want to raise his prestige. The parents of the young lady must know he's a boy. You might also call him pasha. What's to stop you?"

"Why are you making so much noise?" asked Galal, very disturbed.

"My dear Galal," said Rafik, "the day your father marries there will be no more sleep for you. I just want to give you a warning."

At this news, Galal started as though he'd been bitten by a snake.

"My father going to marry!" he cried. "This is horrible. But how? He's way up in his room; he never goes out."

"He doesn't have to go out. It's Haga Zohra, that daughter of a whore, who's managing the whole affair. She's been visiting him continually"

"Don't let her go up," said Galal, crushed with astonishment. "Kill her if you have to. Rafik, my brother, I haven't time to do anything about this. But I have faith in you. I beg you, deliver us from this menace. A woman in the house! What a ghastly thought!"

"Don't worry, I'm here," said Rafik.

He looked at Hoda:

"And you, you bitch, if you ever let her in here, I'll strangle you."

"You really pass all limits," said the uncle. "Rafik, I tell you again, this affair is none of your business."

"Do you know," Rafik continued, "what this worthless Haga Zohra is hawking all over town? She's telling everyone our father has diabetes!"

"Diabetes!" said Serag. "But why?"

"Yes, why?" asked Galal, alarmed by this new misfortune.

"I'll explain it to you," said Rafik. "You're too naïve to understand. According to this ignorant woman's powers of reason, it would seem that a man with diabetes is a man who's eaten many sweets in his life. And if a man's eaten many sweets in his life, it doesn't matter who he is. He must be a man of high social rank. Now do you understand?"

Galal burst out with a dull laugh, but stopped at once. He understood that it was no laughing matter, but rather a tragic turn of events.

"But the woman's a fool," said Serag.

"She isn't a fool," said Rafik. "She's an admirable go-between. What parents, pray tell, wouldn't be proud to give their daughter to a man who's got such a glorious disease? At least it proves that he hasn't eaten only bread and bad cheese."

"Once more, my dear Rafik, save us from this misery," said Galal. "I count on you and name you guardian of our sleep. Show us what you're worth. You've studied—you're almost an engineer."

"I don't have to be an engineer to know how to slice Haga Zohra into a thousand little pieces. You can count on me."

"You're a brave man!" said Galal, reassured.

"My children," said Uncle Mustapha, "don't interfere in this. Your father is master here. If he decides on something, it's his own business."

"Uncle Mustapha, it's not possible. You want to kill us!" said

Galal. "A woman in the house! As if this girl weren't bad enough."

During this discussion, Hoda had prudently remained silent. Old Hafez's marriage had given rise to endless disputes, and she hadn't managed to escape the consequences. She was worried about the future. She got up silently, gathered the dirty plates, and carried them to the kitchen.

Uncle Mustapha didn't speak, but he was busy thinking. Not able to make himself respected, he was careful to defend his brother's decisions. Old Hafez's permanent absence gave him a right to authority. Unfortunately, he used it badly and had become the constant butt of his nephews. Uncle Mustapha suffered to find himself reduced to this subordinate role. But he couldn't do anything to change his situation. Actually, he was very fond of this quiet house and found himself strangely at home there. He now slept as much as the others. Only sometimes he remembered his old happy bachelor's existence and was seized with regret. He gave vent to several sighs of unexpected feeling and looked vaguely around him. These sighs of Uncle Mustapha always gave the impression of an unjust and terrible fate that darkened his existence past the limits of mere weariness.

"Uncle Mustapha," said Rafik, "you should go on the radio. Then your sighs would be heard around the world. I like your sighs; it's as if the world should be bored along with you."

"I don't understand your insolence. What's this new idea?"

"Simply," said Rafik, "I think it's a shame that such beautiful sighs should be lost to strangers. I'm sure the radio would pay you well."

Uncle Mustapha, in reply to this flippancy, gave several more of his singular sighs and became silent.

"You're right to sigh, Uncle Mustapha," said Galal. "It's horrible to wait like this. Where did that girl go?"

"What are you waiting for?" asked Rafik.

"I'm waiting for dessert. And I haven't time."

"You're in a hurry?"

"Yes, I'm in a hurry," said Galal.

After a minute, Hoda came back with a plate filled with oranges and put it on the table.

"I'll take mine with me," said Galal. "I'll eat it in bed. I guess I'll take two: one for dinner, too. I don't think I'll be able to eat with you tonight. I've wasted enough time in this dining room."

He got up and went toward the door. Suddenly he came back.

"I don't have to tell you not to make any noise. Come to bed. What are you doing here awake? On my honor, you're all vicious. Goodbye!"

"Adieu," said Rafik. "And don't forget to write. We're always anxious to hear from you."

IV

It was the sacred hour of siesta; the house was silent as though it were buried at the very depth of silence. Sometimes, a noise of dishes, imperceptible, muffled, laid itself upon the motionless air, like a cry lost in crossing the heaviness of sleep. Rafik, stretched on his bed, was not asleep. His eyes wide open in the gloom, he kept awake with meticulous care, exhausting himself in the unequal struggle against drowsiness. He was waiting for Haga Zohra, the go-between whose intrigues threatened to throw the house into irreparable chaos. He had decided that his father's marriage must not take place; because of this, he hadn't slept for several days. It was an act of daring, almost of folly, and Rafik was afraid of succumbing to his fatigue, of failing at the crucial moment. Sweat dripped from his forehead as he fought the pernicious languor that was taking hold of his limbs, this heavy inertia that crept through him. Already, he had begun to suffer. He was getting stiff and raised himself on his elbows, panting. He heard his own breathing and was alarmed; he had almost awakened Galal who slept in the next bed, his face turned toward the wall, completely shrouded in his quilt. Not a breath marred his sleep that seemed like death. Rafik admired this tremendous anesthesia that no anxiety could disturb. It was almost a comatose state, a stupor. Galal had had no choice; his sleep was not a desire to escape from a world that didn't please him. He even ignored that there was a world outside, full of unhappiness, menacing and greedy. He abandoned himself to sleep naturally, without cares, as to a simple and joyous thing.

Rafik, on the contrary, always had with him the vision of a world of degradation and misery, and had chosen sleep as a refuge. He could feel at peace only behind the shelter of these walls, barricaded against the fatal presence of other beings and things. Around the house ranged a multitude of wrecks with human faces; their nearness was horrible to him. He recalled with terror the times when he used to go out, those chance contacts with the world of men; they were all murderers. He had an unbelievable hatred for them. When still very young he had learned to appreciate the value of the monotonous but sublime existence that his father's house offered. This security, rid of all contingencies, he owed to old Hafez, who had always maintained an atmosphere of passivity around him. Rafik always respected his father for the one noble idea he had found in life, and when, at a certain period, old Hafez had forced him to sacrifice his love of a woman, Rafik had not hesitated, in spite of the suffering it had cost him, to obey his father's will. Old Hafez had been right. Rafik was grateful and blessed him for saving him in time. But now it was his father who was about to ruin this security so painfully acquired by many generations. Rafik rebelled; he felt offended and betrayed.

The woman whom Rafik had loved, at the time when he went out in the world, was a young prostitute who lived in an old dilapidated house near the highway. The quarter referred to her as

"Imtissal, the students' friend," because she only recruited her admirers among the youth of the universities. A whole clientele, scarcely past puberty, crowded to her door. Rafik had sometimes visited her with the other students. In the beginning, Imtissal had scarcely paid any attention to him; he was a customer like the others. Then came a day when she began to treat him differently and refused the money he gave her. Rafik thereupon conceived a certain pride that led him to believe he was an extraordinary being. Imtissal seemed to find a strange pleasure in making love to him. Rafik was never able to forget this time of discovery of the savageness of the flesh. Imtissal began to love him with incredible passion that was almost hysteria. She no longer received her numerous admirers, passing the days waiting for him; she became devouringly faithful. After a few months of this violent love Rafik decided he would marry Imtissal and bring her to live, with him at the house.

When he told his father of his resolution, old Hafez became intractable; he formally opposed it. His son must either leave the house or renounce his insane plan. Rafik's first impulse was to leave and marry Imtissal. However he needed money to live. What could he do? Work! The word was so painful he couldn't bring himself to pronounce it. He deliberated a long time, tortured between his real passion and the vicissitudes of a life where sleep and tranquility would be banished forever. Finally, he renounced his love; no joy of the flesh was worth the sacrifice of his repose. He announced his father's refusal to Imtissal; he confessed his decision to separate from her. It was an unforgettable scene.

This adventure had taken place two years earlier, but Rafik had never forgotten the intensity of those carnal moments. The memory of them burned in him like a devouring flame. The image of Imtissal haunted him even in his sleep. Since their break, she had refused to see him. She had gone back to her old life as a prostitute, and the young students had come back to knock at her door. Rafik kept informed of everything she did; he had learned that she had had a bastard child, whose father she didn't even know. She was raising it herself, in the single room in which she made love.

What tormented Rafik above all was not his separation from Imtissal, but rather the misunderstanding that existed between them. Imtissal had only understood one thing: that Rafik had ceased to love her. He had never had time to make her understand his real motives for leaving her. She had suddenly begun calling him a pimp, because he had told her he never wanted to work. Without even attempting to listen to him, she had screamed like a madwoman, then had thrown him out, showering him with curses.

Rafik wanted to see her one more time; he wanted to try to explain the beauty of this peaceful existence he had chosen above her love. A few days before, he had charged Hoda to go to her and ask her to see him. But Hoda had told him, just before lunch, of the failure of this overture. Imtissal refused to see him. From that moment, Rafik had been thinking of the one means left to approach Imtissal: to go to her house without warning and thus force her to hear him. He resolved to go out some evening and do this. But would she admit him? He was anguished at the thought of this meeting. However, it was too strong for him; he had to try a last explanation with Imtissal. Perhaps he would be able to make her understand that he had never ceased to love her, that this had nothing to do with love; he was simply incapable of leaving his father's house, that shelter which protected him from the ugliness of the world. To tell her all men were murderers, and that he was afraid of them—she would surely take him for a fool. No matter! In any case, after this decisive explanation he would be calmer. Because ever since this drama of love had slipped between him and his sleep, he hadn't been able to taste fully of his quietude. The ghost of Imtissal, vindictive and murderous, always stood before him, an obstacle.

Rafik rose up from the bed, left his room and crossed the hall. In the kitchen, little Hoda was scampering about like a mouse; Rafik slipped noiselessly into the dining room. His plan to intercept Haga Zohra and keep her from seeing his father hadn't left him for a moment. For this purpose the dining room was the best lookout. From the wide-open hallway door, Rafik could watch the wooden staircase that led up to the next floor. Thus, when Haga Zohra came, he could hardly miss seeing her. And then, there was the couch. Rafik could lie down while he waited for this vile go-between. He resisted the couch for the moment; it was still too soon. He would run the risk of falling asleep at once. He must give proof of his endurance. Without it all his laborious maneuvers would have been for nothing. Rafik sighed and called all the energy of which he was capable to his aid. Then he went to the window and looked at the sleeping alley. At this hour, everyone in the house across the way was asleep. It was a three story building, newly constructed, its walls unplastered, with the forbidding look of a prison. Rafik had only seen men there; the women must have hidden themselves, peeking out from behind the blinds. These bourgeois families, with their prejudices and barbarous customs, no doubt forbade their females to show themselves outside. Rafik thought he'd like to sleep with one of them. But that was dangerous, and then they'd be ugly. He gave it up without regret. After a moment a child appeared; he was coming up the other side of the street, playing with a hoop. It was an iron hoop, very heavy, and the child was having trouble rolling it on the uneven ground. He soon disappeared at the turning of the alley, shouting in triumph.

Rafik began to feel again the ravages of this unwonted watch. His eyelids burned, his legs were getting weak. That he had to miss his siesta because of this cursed Haga Zohra was an unbearable torment. This couldn't go on long; in a minute he would have to lie down on the sofa. Leaning against the window and turning his head, he stiffened himself with all his might against sleep. He had the impression of swimming against the current in the middle of a river of treacherous eddies. From time to time, in a supreme effort, he managed to free himself; he raised his head and breathed deeply. Then, again, he found himself plunged into the depths of an annihilating sweetness. The waves of an immense, seductive sleep covered him. Once again he came to the surface to breathe. Suddenly a distant noise reached him; he thought he was dreaming, shook himself, then listened attentively. The noise became more distinct, louder, the deaf murmur of a crowd on the march. Rafik heard them approach slowly, and soon he could see a strange procession passing in front of the window.

It was a man burdened with chains, surrounded by a mob of clamoring children. Some of them marched backwards in front of him, to watch him the better. The man carrying the chains had the stature of a giant, and long hair that fell in curls to his shoulders. A huge beard hid his black face streaming with sweat. His breast was naked and his waist bound with a sort of loin cloth of rags. The ends of the chains were wound round his ankles, as if to weigh down his steps and give him a pathetic grandeur. He looked like a galley slave escaped from some wild and distant prison. With an enormous stone he hit himself on the chest above the heart. The blows were spaced far apart, and each time he raised his arm, the crowd of children became silent in anxious expectation. At the spot where the rock struck him, the skin was only a cracked and greenish crust. The man punctuated each blow with a muffled grumble and some indistinct words like an invocation. He played his role of penitent sinner with a tragic magnificence. Sometimes, from a window, someone threw him some money; the man gathered it up and slipped it into a leather pouch hanging around his loins.

Rafik had seen this creature several times before, and even, while still a child, had followed him in his rounds through the alleys. But was this the same man? There were numbers of them who had adopted this system of spectacular begging. They had formed a wild sect and were proud of these tortures they inflicted on themselves to make people pity them. Rafik was horrified. These diabolical means to which men were reduced to live seemed to him like the extreme limit of a universal nightmare. The man loaded with chains looked toward the window, slowly raised his arm and beat the heavy stone against his chest. During this brief moment, his gaze fell on Rafik standing at the window. Rafik closed his eyes and stood without moving, the keen look of the man planted in him like a knife. He waited a long time till the noise of the crowd grew distant, then he opened his eyes.

Again silence and peace. Rafik felt ill. He was tired; he trembled with humiliation and disgust. Instinctively he moved toward the couch and lay down. The spectacle of men devoted to the vilest misery depressed him as though he had been caught in their ruin. He had tried to insure himself against such contacts, had raised walls between himself and this degraded and subject humanity. He didn't want to be a party to such abjectness. He felt outraged; he felt a physical repulsion even to witness such insane brutality. It was really a butchery; everywhere the same people, stupefied, jostling, carried along like a herd of buffaloes by the same everlasting lies.

Rafik breathed deeply, stretched and tried to forget the horrible eyes of the man with the chains. One more thing to forget.

How many times had he tried to forget the hideous sights that were always before him? It was useless to try to hide them; the poisonous vapors filtered through the cracks of his hiding place. He remembered he had resolved to go seek out Imtissal and felt a desperate terror.

"It will be the last time I go out," he told himself. He lay motionless, like a fox in his lair, waiting for Haga Zohra. There was nothing but silence, an impalpable silence, empty of all substance. Suddenly a voice echoed from the next floor. It was old Hafez calling Hoda, and his words seemed smothered by the monstrous silence. Rafik leaped up, ran to the door and looked into the hallway. He saw Hoda, barefoot, start hurriedly up the stairs. The young girl, shocked to see him, stopped short.

"Come here, girl!"

Hoda came back down the steps and up to him timidly.

"I know why he's calling you," said Rafik. "He wants to know if Haga Zohra is here. Tell him she hasn't come and that she isn't coming anymore. I'll strangle you, I warn you, if you ever let that woman in the house. Besides, I'm here; I'll wait."

"It's not my affair," said Hoda. "What have I got to do with it? Why pick on me?"

"I know he's promised you some money. And you want to make us all miserable, filthy girl!"

Hoda was ready to cry. She knew Rafik's brutality, his rudeness and his violence. She lowered her eyes, assumed a look of humility, and resigned herself to his worst.

"I don't want money," she said. "I don't want anything. Have I asked for anything? I just do what I'm told."

"Then do what I tell you," shouted Rafik.

"Ssh!" whispered Hoda. "You'll wake everyone."

Rafik stopped, disconcerted at the thought that everyone was asleep. He who was always so careful of others' sleep—what had happened to him? Exhaustion had made him lose control of himself. But there was something else. Rafik realized that he wanted Hoda, and that his desire had been born the same instant she whispered to him to be quiet. The silence was erotic. It carried the heavy odor of an oppressing voluptuousness. He caught Hoda by the throat and tried to drag her to the couch.

"Come," he said.

She shook her head, struggling to free herself.

"Not now," she said. "I haven't time. My master's calling. I'll come back later …"

But Rafik wasn't listening to her. He held her by her waist, blindly pressed her against him, in a mad desire for sleep rather than lust. Hoda fought silently. She knew what was coming; he was always like this with her. Rafik was already searching under her dress, trying to touch her.

She felt his fingers hunting in her; a shiver ran over her body and she began to struggle more desperately. She felt that Rafik was drowning and that his movements were weak and without desire. In fact, Rafik was already tired of the battle. His head fell back, he yawned; his tenseness left him, he felt himself falling into an abyss of unconsciousness. Hoda, with an abrupt movement, managed to escape his grasp. She ran up the stairs.

"I'll strangle you, daughter of a whore!"

He waited a moment at the bottom of the stairway; he could hear his father's cries cursing Hoda for being late. Then, he fell back into a heavy, devouring silence. Rafik was still panting from frustrated desire; he had lost all feeling in his legs, his head was spinning sickeningly. To sleep! But he was too furious with himself to go back to the couch. He needed to talk to someone.

V

Serag wasn't asleep, he was only resting. When Rafik entered the room, he opened his eyes and was astounded to see his brother up at this sacred hour of the siesta.

"Why are you awake? Have you gone crazy?"

"I'm not crazy," replied Rafik. "Worse than that. You don't seem to remember. While you sleep, I alone have been trying to do something about the unhappiness that is menacing us."

"What unhappiness are you talking about?"

"You still haven't understood anything! It's true—you don't think of anything but running up and down the roads. However, your father's marriage should give you something to worry about. It's a real calamity for us all. Serag, my brother, our peace is threatened, don't you understand?"

"Then you really believe in this marriage?"

"Certainly I believe it. Your father insists on it, if only for spite. It's a long time since he's annoyed someone, and now he can. I'm sure he'll do it as soon as possible."

He sat on the foot of the bed, pulling his legs under him, and buried his face in his hands. The shutters hadn't been closed and a luminous day flooded the room. Rafik hated this cold light that enveloped him like a shroud.

"How can you sleep in that light?" he asked.

"I wasn't sleeping," said Serag. "I'm trying to get used to the day. I don't want to live in the dark."

Rafik sighed and didn't answer. His face in his hands, he seemed to meditate. He hadn't yet recovered from his attempt upon Hoda and a vague excitement persisted in him. Serag looked at him with amused sympathy. He realized Rafik was fighting against sleep and was curious to know his reactions. Would he be able to hold out long? He had never seen his brother exert such an effort against the poisons of sleep. It was like a miracle—a miracle of a man suspended above a precipice, holding himself in the air by his will alone.

"What do you plan to do?"

Rafik uncovered his face, blinked, and said in a sarcastic tone:

"If I'm awake at this hour, my dear Serag, it's not for my own pleasure, believe me. It's a question of not letting Haga Zohra in the house. Without her help, your father will never be able to get married. It's very simple. Thus, as you see, I'm waiting for Haga Zohra, to throw her out."

"Then you're going to spend your time waiting for her?"

"Yes, I'll wait as long as I have to."

"But this could last for months."

"All right! I'll wait months—years even—if I have to."

"You're a hero!" said Serag. "I didn't think you were capable of such a sacrifice."

"This sacrifice is going to save our lives," said Rafik. "You can't imagine what it would be like to have a woman around us. In a few days we'd be reduced to slavery."

He became silent; Serag didn't know what to think of his

brother's attitude. That Rafik should give up his siesta, because of this story of a marriage, seemed insane to him. Something else must have pushed him to this extremity. Perhaps hatred for his father.

"You were also going to bring a woman into the house," he said. "Have you forgotten? You've borne a grudge against your father ever since your episode with Imtissal."

Rafik started; he seemed to have suddenly lost his torpor. He turned on Serag, looking at him threateningly.

"That's not true," he said, "I've no grudge against him. I've known he was right for a long time. You don't know all the respect I have for him. I admire him for the kind of life he's led and has surrounded us with. He's never wanted to get mixed up with the world, he's never tried to increase his fortune. And above all, he's always despised other men. All the members of our family were like servants before him, even though some of them were richer than he is. It's his disdain to mix in the affairs of the world that has always pleased me. That's what gives us this quiet and this marvelous idleness. How could I hate him? But now he wants to ruin everything. And I won't allow it."

"I don't see how this marriage will ruin our lives," said Serag.

"Why can't you understand! This woman can destroy us. A woman will want clothes, jewels—I don't know what all. One day she could be possessed by the devil and decide she must organize a séance to cast him out. You see us sleeping in the middle of all those mad dancers!"

Serag began to laugh. Rafik's idea struck him as a tremendous joke.

"Don't laugh," said Rafik severely. "This is very serious. Your father can lose his last penny in this adventure. We may be forced to go to work!"

"Well!" said Serag. "I ask nothing better."

"O idiot! You'll repent those words."

"I assure you Rafik, I want to work."

"You want to work. I don't know where you ever got the idea, You are without doubt either a monster or an imbecile. In any case, you're certainly not one of this family."

"I want to work," said Serag, with a tone of despair. "And also to leave this house."

"On my honor! You're an ingrate. If you weren't my brother, I'd let you go through with this madness. But I pity you. Which reminds me, what's happening at your factory?"

"The factory's always the same," replied Serag. "I've been to see it again this morning. No one seems to want to finish it."

"Then finish it yourself," said Rafik. "There's a good job. What are you complaining about?"

"You're making fun of me, damn you!"

"Listen Serag, I'm not making fun of you. I'm only trying to lead you off a bad road. Believe me, work is no good for you or any of us."

"Maybe," said Serag. "But I don't want to keep living like this."

"You're young. I really do pity you. You still don't know what kind of factory it is?"

"Do you know?"

"Yes," said Rafik. "When I was studying to be an engineer, we used to visit factories. They were huge, unhealthy, sad buildings. I spent the most painful moments of my life in them. I've seen the men who work in those factories; only they weren't still men. Their misery was written on their faces. If I left my studies, it was solely because I didn't want to be the head of that horde of sufferers."

Serag shivered at this lugubrious speech. He closed his eyes and saw his romantic dream of work crumbling, broken in the maze of immeasurable sadness. Work could only be a damnation and a suffering. Serag was silent; he was the prey of a dull uneasiness.

During a long moment, there was silence, then they heard a soft creaking. Rafik jumped off the bed, opened the door and glanced down the hall.

"No," he said. "No one."

"You thought it was Haga Zohra?" asked Serag.

"Yes, I thought it was. Never mind; I should move, otherwise I'll fall asleep. What misery! and I can't count on any of you. Your brother Galal is sleeping peacefully. He hasn't even tried to think about the danger he's in. But pretty soon he won't be able to sleep."

"How are you going to keep him from sleeping?" asked Serag. "Nothing can wake Galal. I'll bet he isn't even thinking about this. He's already forgotten."

"He won't forget for long," said Rafik. "I've had enough of seeing him peacefully relaxed, while I kill myself waiting. He'll have to help me."

"By Allah I don't see Galal leaving his bed to watch for Haga Zohra. You're crazy if you expect it."

"Believe me, I'll get him out of his bed. He hasn't realized what this fatal marriage means. When he sees, he won't sleep anymore either."

Rafik began to walk around the room; from time to time he stopped in front of the window. Serag's room was at the back of the house, and looked out on a vacant lot where some scrubby bushes were growing among all kinds of rubbish.

In the middle of the lot was a dwarf palm, dried up and fruitless; men used to come to it to piddle against its trunk. At this moment, a child was squatting by it, his raised galabiah revealing his nakedness, urinating dejectedly. Farther away, one could see the winding line of houses profiled against the fields. Rafik was content; he had just rid Serag of his illusions. He would have liked to disgust him with work forever; it was an invaluable service. All his repulsion for the workaday lives of men had risen in his throat. He came back and said with malicious cruelty:

"Do you know, my dear Serag, that there are countries where men get up at four o'clock in the morning to work in the mines?"

"Mines!" said Serag. "It isn't true; you want to frighten me."

He was deeply impressed. This upsetting conception of work that Rafik had inoculated him with, drop by drop, like a poison, finally convinced him it was all true. He would have liked to learn more, but Rafik didn't speak and had begun pacing the room again.

'Tell me, Rafik, my brother, that's not true what you just said?"

"What's not true?"

"That in some countries the men get up at four in the morning to work in the mines."

"It's true all right," said Rafik. "We haven't any mines here yet, but they'll come. Someone will discover them. They'll discover anything to force men to work and make beasts of them."

"But isn't there some other kind of work?"

Rafik gave a short laugh. It amused him to see Serag frightened as a child.

"Don't be afraid. There aren't any mines here yet. But men can do anything. They'll find a way of discovering mines, even here where there aren't any."

"Who told you?"

"No one. But I know men better than you do. They won't wait long, I tell you, to spoil this fertile valley and turn it into a hell. That's what they call progress. You've never heard that word? Well, when a man talks to you about progress, you can be sure that he wants to subjugate you. In any case, for the moment, you've a magnificent security around you. And you want to go out! You're mad; you don't know what's waiting for you."

Rafik had stopped again in front of the window. He said no more and looked at the stunted palm balancing its branches in the heavy air. The child had left; an old man wearing a turban had taken his place. He personified humanity, squatting and blissful in his excrement. Rafik turned and came over to the bed.

"Tell me, I've asked you all day what news you have of the outside. Really, I would like to know about the weather. Is it very cold? Is there too much dust?"

"Why all these questions?"

"I have to go out," said Rafik. "But I'm not yet completely decided. It's only some business."

"You, Rafik, you're going out?"

"Yes, I'm going out. But believe me, it's not to look for work. And now, sleep well, I'm going to try to get us out of our troubles."

He left the room and went back to the dining room. He was still preoccupied with the same idea: to keep Haga Zohra from seeing his father. He lay down on the couch and waited. But he didn't wait long. Sleep fell on him like a stone and crushed him.

VI

Since Rafik bad told him there were countries where men got up at four in the morning to work in the mines, Serag had been trying to do as much himself. He had discovered an alarm clock in a closet, and had had it repaired with the intention of using it. As he slept alone in his room, he could indulge in this unheard-of whim. However, the first day, the alarm nearly caused a riot in the house. Serag, not yet accustomed to this violent rupture of sleep, had let the clock ring on and on. He thought he was having a nightmare. On waking he had felt himself capable of tremendous activity. But some minutes later, not knowing what to do, he had gone back to sleep. He tried again the next day, and the next, having taken care to roll the clock in a towel to muffle the noise of the alarm. But these numerous attempts continued to be as unfruitful as the first. Hadn't Rafik deliberately lied in order to frighten him? Serag now had doubts about the possibility of anyone's getting up so early. It seemed improbable to him that sane men would go to work in the mines at this unwholesome hour. What could force them into such madness?

However, Rafik had studied at the engineering school, so undoubtedly he should know. With him, though, you never knew when he was, laughing at you or telling the truth. In his sarcasms you could only see a deranged world pursued by unhappiness, a world swarming with bloody assassins.

While this was going on, to keep himself busy, Serag tried to find a solution for the problem of Abou Zeid's shop; this passed the time and thus he could feel that he wasn't completely inactive. Several ideas came to him, but he rejected them all, finding them ordinary or too easy. He wanted to find something supremely original, something that would amaze Abou Zeid and, at the same time, show him he was a member of a family of decision and refinement. But the idea hadn't come yet. Serag was in no hurry. He reflected on the matter slowly, with circumspection, sure of uncovering a great idea in the end.

Serag hadn't been out of the house since his last trip to the unfinished factory. He had to hoard his energy before undertaking a new excursion outside. Now, however, he felt himself in shape again, well disposed after several days of sleep, and he had decided to go and take still another look at the factory. To be sure, he didn't really count on seeing it already finished, but it was a great consolation for him to visit the spot where he should have been working. He found a comfort and a feeling of action there that enabled him to survive the atmosphere of his home.

Stretched out on his bed, Serag looked toward the window and beyond the window at the blue sky, without a trace of clouds, where the sun burned radiantly. It was a spring day, a spring day that already carried a fatal warmth. Serag was rejoicing at the idea of the long walk to the factory. He thought of the child with the slingshot, saying to himself that perhaps he might see him again. He had an absorbing desire to find him—that child could he so useful to him! He had never forgiven himself for letting him leave without asking for all the details of his vagabond life. Serag thought of him as a skilled traveller; he was thirsty to hear all about his many pilgrimages around the city. With what a strange passion he had chased the birds! Serag had never sensed such a feeling of power in another human being. It was as if the child carried all the weight of the world and, at the same time, defended himself from it with a disdainful carelessness. He had seen so many things, met so many men, Serag promised himself, if he saw him again, to ask his advice about how he could live a fierce and passionate existence. His competence in the matter would be a great help.

He got out of bed, walked toward the closet and opened it. He took out his red woollen sweater, his football shoes, and began to dress.

"You're going out?"

The door had just opened; Serag turned, saw Hoda, and became provoked. The young girl gently closed the door and walked into the room on tiptoe. She repeated, in a whisper:

"Are you going out?'

"Yes, I'm going out," said Serag.

"Wait for me," said Hoda. "I'll finish the dishes and we can go out together."

"That's impossible," said Serag. "I have some urgent business; I can't wait."

"That's not true," said Hoda. "The truth is you don't want me to go. You don't love me."

She spoke in a childish voice, full of naïve reproach that moved Serag and troubled him. Her love for him was a hindrance to his projects for escape and an active life. He was angry for letting himself be affected by this amorous and obstinate little girl. It was a weakness worse than sleep that he couldn't bear to see her suffer. He said, with a profound gentleness:

"But I do love you, you know it well. Only I haven't time. I have to go out right now."

She became sad and pouted; she didn't believe him. She knew be had no urgent business, that it was only his desire to roam that took him outside.

"You ought to sleep," she said.

"I've slept enough. I have to go out. Don't you understand?"

"What are you going to do outside? I'm afraid for you when you're outside."

"You're only a little girl. Why should you be afraid? All men don't stay inside and sleep. You don't know anything about life."

"But you're not like other men," she said. "I'm afraid for you."

"You're crazy! What could happen to me? Do you know, Hoda, there are countries where men get up at four in the morning to work in the mines?"

"That's another of your inventions."

"No it isn't. Rafik told me."

"It isn't true," said Hoda, "He was lying."

"Do you think so?" said Serag. "Anyhow, it's very difficult. I tried and couldn't do it."

"You tried to get up at four in the morning? What for? There aren't any mines around here."

"No, but Rafik said there would be soon. Anyhow, I have to train myself."

"Hush," said Hoda. "You really frighten me. Won't you wait for me?"

She had a little girl's stubborn attachment for him—a sort of vicious and troubled love. For him she accepted the vexations of her situation; thinking of him, she submitted to all the outrages and insults. She knew he wanted to leave the house, and she didn't know how to stop him. If he would take her with him, she would leave gladly.

She came over to Serag, pressed herself against him, and put her arms around him. He was tall so she had to raise her head to look at him. She looked supplicating and tender. Serag couldn't help smiling at her.

"Kiss me," she said.

"I haven't time. I have to go, I tell you. And I don't want to tire myself, I've a long walk ahead of me."

She held him more closely.

"Kiss me," she begged.

Serag put his arms around her neck and began to kiss her mouth. He felt her tremble, and knew he couldn't get away until he had made love to her. He loosened his embrace and sat on the bed. Hoda joined him, rubbed herself against him coaxingly, her eyes brilliant with a malicious light. She turned on her back and waited, submissive, for the approach of pleasure. She was smiling vaguely, her eyelids lowered, her face taut with expectation. A long moment she remained inert, not daring to move. Serag raised her dress, uncovering her slender brown legs. Hoda looked at Serag, then at her legs, as if they belonged to someone else. The pleasure had not yet come; she felt it trembling in her like a wounded bird. Serag moved his hand gently up her thigh, reached the sensitive spot of her flesh and lingered there. She gave a soft cry, caught him to her with all her strength and forced him to lie beside her.

He softly bit the tips of her breasts that had slipped through her dress. She let him enter her, her face happy and mischievous. Soon Serag's head weighted her chest; she felt him falling asleep.

"Do you know," she asked, "that Galal promised to give me five piastres if I'd let him see my breasts?"

Serag drew back, looking at her stupidly.

"He promised you five piastres!" he said. "He's fooling you, he hasn't any money."

"Even if he had some," said Hoda, "do you think I'd do it?"

"I don't know," said Serag. "Maybe he could force you to."

"If he forced me," said Hoda, "that wouldn't be the same thing. Besides, he never would."

"Why? Hasn't he ever made you embrace him?"

"No," said Hoda. "He tried, but he's too lazy. He'd rather sleep."

"Then I don't understand. Why would he want to see your breasts?"

"No doubt that would give him pleasure," said Hoda. "Sometime he wants to enjoy himself without getting too tired. Aren't you jealous?"

Serag smiled and looked at Hoda.

"No, I am not jealous."

Hoda didn't say anything; she looked disappointed. She had wanted to make him jealous.

"The one who always forces me is Rafik," she said. "I don't know how to get away from him."

"Don't you like Rafik?" asked Serag. "He's really remarkable. Do you know he's been spending his time watching in the dining room to keep Haga Zohra from seeing my father. He's been waiting for her for days. He'll surely end by getting sick."

"I know," said Hoda, "He hasn't only been waiting for Haga Zohra. Most of the time he's waiting for me too."

"Does that annoy you?" asked Serag. "He's nice, Rafik. Why don't you like him?"

"I only like you," said Hoda. "And you're mean to me."

"I'm not mean," said Serag. "I'm just thinking about other things."

"What are you thinking about?" asked Hoda. "By Allah! You're crazier than the others. I'm so unhappy!"

"Go away," said Serag. "I have to leave. I'm late already."

"Don't go too far," said Hoda.

She got up from the bed, smoothed her dress, and went out of the room silently.

Serag closed the gate to the garden and walked toward the highway. He was in a bad mood, felt weak, and cursed himself for giving in to this mood of Hoda's. Now he didn't have the energy to go as far as the factory; he'd have to put it off until another time. He realized that this girl was as pernicious to him as sleep. Her attachment for him was going to compromise his attempt for a free, industrious life. It was one more fetter to his dream of running away from his father's house. How could he get free of her? Still, she was only a child, and Serag felt sorry for her. She was unhappy, he knew; she would be even more unhappy when he left.

Serag reached the highway; he had decided to go see Abou Zeid at his shop. He wished to submit several rather banal ideas to the peanut vendor that might give his mediocre business a lift. Thus, at least, his afternoon wouldn't be entirely lost. It was warm, almost hot; Serag perspired and panted slightly, his eyes blinded by the glare. The sun burned everywhere, and the houses, on both sides of the road, seemed painted with large swaths of light. Serag was walking unsteadily, feeling as though he had ventured into an overwhelming brightness, full of invisible hazards. His hands felt damp in his pockets; he pulled them out and wiped them on his pants. Then he walked on, his arms swinging, his mind empty, his eyes fixed on the ground. He rarely met anyone on the road; it was too early. Serag was happy not to meet anyone. He didn't want to talk, and then people always looked at him so strangely. They knew all his family, and smiled foolishly when they saw him coming. Serag was mortified every time. Suddenly he saw Mimi come out of an alley and hurry toward him, smiling. Mimi held his dog Semsen on a leash—a wretched animal, thin and dirty, that never left him.

"Hello," said Mimi. "I haven't seen you for a long time. How are you?"

"I don't go out very much," said Serag. "Are you taking a walk? How's your dog?"

"He's a dirty beast," said Mimi. "He gives me a lot of trouble. Listen: I wanted to see you."

"Really," said Serag. "What about?"

"I wanted to talk to you," said Mimi. "I've been wandering around your house every day hoping to see you. But I didn't have any luck."

"Is it very important?" asked Serag.

Mimi didn't answer. He looked at Serag out of the corner of his eye, with a gleam of lust.

"Oh! it's nothing very important," he said. "I really just wanted to see you."

"I'm glad I ran into you," said Serag.

"Really?" asked Mimi.

"Of course," said Serag. "I like your dog very much."

"May I walk with you for a minute?" asked Mimi.

"Please do," said Serag.

They began to walk along the side of the road, in the shade. Mimi held his head over his shoulder and smiled with ecstasy. He was still ogling Serag out of the corner of his eye. He was an odd young man, dressed with a studied elegance, with doubtful but refined manners. His plucked eyebrows and eyes darkened with grease gave him an equivocal, insinuating look. He walked daintily, lightly swinging his hips. From time to time he drew a handful of roasted watermelon seeds out of his jacket pocket and ate them with exquisite care.

"Would you like some?" he asked Serag.

"No thanks," said Serag. "I don't like them."

"You should, they're delicious. Unfortunately, they're difficult to eat if one doesn't know how to go about it."

"I've never learned how to do it," said Serag. "No one ever eats them at our house."

"Yes, it's not easy for you," said Mimi. "You don't ever dare try it. You probably only like what's easy to eat. You don't want to tire yourselves too much."

"Oh no!" said Serag. "It's just that no one likes them."

"I understand," said Mimi, "You don't have to explain to me. And above all, don't be angry about what I just said."

"I'm not angry," said Serag.

"Good," said Mimi. "I'm so happy to have met you."

He fluttered his eyelashes and smiled; he had beautiful red lips, rather full. Serag was terribly embarrassed. Mimi hadn't yet explained why he had wanted to see him, but he knew him enough to guess the reason. He broke the silence:

"Do you still paint?"

"Yes," said Mimi. "I even think I've succeeded in doing some extraordinary canvases. Someone wants to buy them; but I don't want to sell."

Mimi was a pupil at the Beaux Arts; he was going to be a painter and considered himself a great artist. No one had ever seen his paintings, but he claimed they were masterpieces. His family took him at his word; as for his many friends, they ridiculed him openly. In all the quarter he had a reputation for being rather bizarre, and for having his own unique morals.

"Did they offer you much money?" asked Serag.

"Of course," said Mimi. "But I don't care about money. I paint only for art."

"That's very beautiful," said Serag. "You should be happy."

"Only art interests me," said Mimi. "That's why I'm so interested in your family. You too, in your own way, are artists."

"I don't understand," said Serag. "We aren't artists, you're mistaken. We don't do anything at all."

"But that's just it," said Mimi. "This strange idleness, in my opinion, is a supreme and distinguished art."

"You're very nice," said Serag. "But I assure you, you're mistaken. We're not artists."

Mimi was silent. He was content to have expressed himself. After some lectures on the Occident, he had formed a rather cloudy notion of modern aesthetics. His own ambiguous morals had the same origin. Mimi firmly believed that a true artist must be a pederast by nature. When a friend had asked him what he thought of the philosophy of a celebrated contemporary writer, Mimi had answered: "What do you want me to think? He's a married man!" His reply had pleased him enormously. He would have loved to tell it to Serag, but he had never asked him. No matter! it would do for another time. He moved his tongue over his lips and smiled easily. He seemed to have lost himself entirely in his unwholesome reveries.

"Come here, you dirty little dog! Aren't you ashamed—a female."

Semsen rubbed himself against Mimi's legs, sheepish and docile. The female dog did not move from her place, watching the scene with rather vague astonishment. Mimi kissed Semsen, picked up a stone and threw it at the other dog. She leaped in the air and ran away without trying to understand what had happened. Semsen regretfully watched her leave. He suffered from his abnormal situation. He was a small mongrel with reddish hair and debauched eyes. He was not a pederast by his own taste, but only for fear of displeasing his master. Mimi punished him brutally each time he approached a female. Semsen was resigned to his lot. His desire to follow his normal instinct seemed like a tragic error to him, since it always brought him blows and insults.

Mimi calmed himself; he reprimanded his dog with a feigned brutality.

"Son of a bitch! I should kill you!"

"What astonishes me," said Serag, "is the way you could immediately tell it was a female."

"I can recognize that easily," said Mimi. "The dirty animals; they're rotten and full of fleas."

"It's still astonishing," said Serag. "I can't ever tell."

They walked on a moment without talking; they were almost alone on the road. From time to time, Mimi turned and threw a furtive look behind. He seemed to be waiting for someone. He put his hand in his pocket and drew out a handful of watermelon seeds. He began to crack them one after the other with a sharp sound. The noise bothered Serag and kept him from dozing. He shook himself and looked around. A cab had just appeared on the road; it came toward them slowly, like a soft dream. It was driven by an enormous driver, who was whipping his horses with fury. In the cab, a huge woman was enthroned on the cushions—a woman of great importance, one would have judged by the monument of her loose flesh. The breeze raised her skirts, revealing her corpulent nudity with cruel lewdness. The two young men gasped.

"Horrible," said Mimi. "Did you see!"

Serag didn't reply; he had stopped in front of Abou Zeid's shop. Mimi's presence upset him; above all, he couldn't bear his voice. Mimi had an insidious and caressing voice, like syrup. Serag felt caught and was aware of a strange sensation in his whole body. He would have liked to lie down by the side of the road to sleep awhile.

Mimi wasn't paying any attention to him. He was possessed by a great exaltation. He became feverish and looked around uneasily every minute. Obviously, he was waiting for something.

Suddenly, he seemed relieved at the sight of a man stopped near a tobacco shop. He was about forty, with curled moustaches and huge rings on his fingers. His tarboosh was tipped over his right ear and he carried a cane in his hand. He gave Mimi a conniving look, then lit a cigarette, puffing the smoke with an easy and innocent air. Mimi smiled at him, turned, and put his arm through Serag's.

"You seem preoccupied," he said. "Are you, by any chance, in love?"

"I'm not in love," said Serag.

Mimi smiled and said ecstatically:

"All love! I couldn't live without love."

Serag didn't answer him. After a minute Mimi said again:

"Tell me: how's your brother Rafik?"

"He's all right," said Serag.

Mimi had been in the same class with Rafik and always favoured him. He loved his rude manners, the harsh sound of his voice, and his pallor of the sensual male. Unfortunately, Rafik had always met Mimi's advances with a stiff and cold disdain. Mimi was profoundly wounded each time, yet his desire grew. He was almost completely happy when he could just see Rafik and delight in his presence. But since Rafik had resolved to stay in the house, Mimi had been left to the torments of the abandoned lover. Actually, his whole conversation with Serag had only been to hear some news about his brother.

"Why doesn't he ever go out?" asked Mimi.

"He doesn't like people," said Serag. "He'd rather stay in the house."

He hates me," said Mimi. "I don't know why. I like him very much."

"I don't think he hates you," said Serag. "You're wrong about that, I'm sure."

"He hates me," said Mimi. "Every time he sees me, and it's scarcely ever now, he tries to avoid me. What have I done to make him hate me? Would you, my dear Serag, do me a favour?"

"With pleasure," said Serag. "What is it?"

"Well, I'd like you to ask Rafik why he doesn't like me. It's very important to me. I'm so fond of him. Will you tell him?"

"I won't forget," said Serag.

Mimi turned and looked behind. The man with the moustaches and the large rings was following them slowly. Mimi came close to Serag and whispered in his ear:

"I'm terribly sorry, but I must leave you. I have to meet someone."

In pronouncing these words, he seemed to confide a momentous secret to Serag.

"I'm very glad to have seen you," he said again, before going away. "Goodbye."

"Goodbye," said Serag.

A group of wan children was standing in front of Abou Zeid's shop; the neighborhood school had just let out for the afternoon. Some little boys and girls, their books under their arms, were buying things and pushing one another around. Abou Zeid was not waiting on them with his usual nonchalance; he seemed a bit frightened by his turbulent clientele. Serag waited until there was no one left, then he went up to Abou Zeid.

"Hello!" he said, "O illustrious merchant!"

"Ah! it's you my son! By Allah! Spare me your sarcasms."

Serag squatted near Abou Zeid and let sleep overcome him. Abou Zeid watched him sleep, and then he too closed his eyes. Behind them, the black beetles took possession of the empty shop.

VII

Old Hafez woke up with a start; he was shivering and bathed in cold sweat. He had just had a bad dream, an endless, terrible dream. He raised the handkerchief tied over his eyes with a feverish movement and shrank back under the covers fearfully. He tried to remember his dream, but it had become confused in his mind. He had only a vague, troubled memory that excited his senile sensuality. After a moment, he grew calmer and looked around. The room was plunged in half darkness, so that he had no idea what the time was. Old Hafez tried to discover the hour by some sign in the room. He glanced around, then stopped before a tray on the table. He'd eaten lunch. Therefore it must be afternoon, and he had just taken his siesta. He pulled off the handkerchief that still bound his forehead and protected him from the disturbing brightness of the day. He couldn't sleep without it.

He sat up in bed and began to think. As usual, his reflections were simple and passionless. But for some time he had been prey to gnawing thoughts; a mute uneasiness was devouring him. This marriage he had resolved upon, at the decline of his life, preoccupied him beyond all reason. It was the desire for renewed youth, and, at the same time, an act of authority. In his solitude, he had imagined this marriage as the last manifestation of his failing will. His unsociable spirit was always toying with all sorts of caprices whose essential aim was to contradict those around him. For some years he had not given an undeniable proof of his bad disposition; his family had begun to forget. Thus before dying, he wanted to leave some ineffaceable evidence of his tyrannical power.

For several days old Hafez had been waiting impatiently for Haga Zohra. She had promised to help him. She was a notorious go-between, and the allure of a profit made her extremely diligent. Old Hafez wasn't worried about that; his worries were elsewhere. He paused in his reflections and listened to the silence of the house. No noise came from the first floor—everywhere the same silence. They must all be asleep. Old Hafez thought bitterly of his children. He hadn't seen them for a long time; sometimes he managed not to see them for months. But through Uncle Mustapha he knew everything that was being plotted against him. Decidedly, they weren't pleased with the idea of his marriage. He also knew Rafik was at the head of the revolt, that he'd sworn to kill Haga Zohra. He had given them too much freedom, and now they thought they could do anything. But he knew how to break them; he would show them he was still master.

Unfortunately, this struggle with his children was only a minor concern. Something else preoccupied him much more—a monstrous affliction. Old Hafez considered this affliction as the only serious obstacle to his marriage. He couldn't even think of it without seeing his dream of a tardy union dissolve at once. He pulled back the covers, raised his nightgown, and examined his lower abdomen worriedly. An enormous hernia protruded like a mountain between his thin legs. It was really horrible. Each time old Hafez looked at his hernia, he was stupefied by its form. Every day it assumed fantastic shapes. Old Hafez was saddened when he uncovered it. He asked himself anxiously how he could dare present a young wife with such a calamity.

He put out a trembling hand and tested the swollen, hard skin with extreme circumspection. Then he began to massage the edges slowly and expertly. Old Hafez watched hopefully to see this stubborn swelling between his legs grow smaller, but it seemed, on the contrary, to enlarge under his hand. It was ridiculous, insane. After some minutes, he gave up his treatment, pulled up the covers, and began to call for Hoda. No one answered. He took a package of cigarettes from under his pillow, drew one out and lit it. Then he called again. This time, he heard Hoda running up the stairs.

"You don't listen when I call you!"

Hoda was panting slightly; she was always afraid when she entered the old man's room. She felt physically ill and wanted to vomit.

"I came up right away," she said.

She lowered her head humbly; her hair was hidden under a scarlet kerchief, bordered with tiny white shells. She watched the old man furtively, waiting for his orders. Sometimes he was completely unreasonable. Most of all, she feared he would make her look at his hernia. Old Hafez frequently showed it to her, simply to watch her reaction. Hoda's obstinate silence usually comforted him, but today it didn't help; he tossed in his bed and groaned:

"Open the window!"

Hoda went to the window and opened it. The rude light invaded the room, and the objects resumed the look of dead things. It was a large room, filled with heavy furniture, tarnished and dusty. Old Hafez felt drowned by this profusion of light; he blinked his eyes and turned to the wall.

"Tell me, girl! Hasn't Haga Zohra come yet?"

"No," said Hoda. "Not yet."

"Are you sure?"

"I'm sure," said Hoda. "I haven't seen her."

He rolled over and squinted at her.

"You're lying, daughter of a bitch! I know my children told you not to let her come up."

"That's not true," said Hoda. "No one has told me anything. I'll bring her up when she comes."

"Listen to me, you little ingrate! Don't forget that I'm the master in this house. You take orders from me alone."

"Yes, master," said Hoda, "I do what you tell me."

"If you don't, I'll throw you out of here. I only keep you out of pity for your mother. Don't try to fool me. As for the children, I can take care of them, even if I don't see them very often."

He moved his hand over his chin, feeling the stiff hairs of his beard.

"And now, get ready to shave me."

Hoda disappeared and came back with a basin of water, putting it on the table. Old Hafez got out of bed, and walked tremulously toward the rocking chair near the window. He was incredibly thin; his nightgown flapped around him. He walked bent over, his legs crooked, weighted down by his hernia. He dropped into the chair, threw back his head, and waited. Hoda began to soap his face. He closed his eyes with satisfaction. He felt a voluptuous pleasure at this freshness on his skin. He had a face of acute angles, cut by an abundant moustache, with edges yellowed by tobacco smoke. It sickened Hoda to touch this decaying, old man's skin. His breath stank, and Hoda, afraid of fainting, strained not to come too close to him.

"What are the children doing?" he asked.

"They aren't doing anything," said Hoda. "They're sleeping."

"It's all they know how to do," said old Hafez. "By Allah! They're beyond hope. Does Serag go out very much?"

"He's been out once or twice," said Hoda.

"That child is crazy! What's he looking for outside?"

Old Hafez had a particular fondness for his youngest son. The boy seemed to him to possess a demon for adventure. He didn't know how to steer him off his dangerous road. Old Hafez felt personally responsible for the difficulties that would not fail to overwhelm Serag if he persisted. He had created an existence of complete repose for him, and here he was, running out of the house with the diabolical idea of looking for work! Surely this generation was inconsiderate and frivolous. He thought he should have a serious talk with Serag. He would show him that his rash scheme was only an absurd and fruitless game. Old Hafez didn't want one of his children to become a tramp on the streets. The honor of the family forbade it.

"You tell Serag I don't want him to go out," he said. "That child is going to be killed one of these days."

"Yes, master," said Hoda. "I'll tell him."

Hoda had finished shaving old Hafez when Uncle Mustapha came to see his brother. He lived on the same floor in an adjoining room.

"I've come to ask you for a cigarette," he said with a forced smile.

"You and the children, you take all my cigarettes," said old Hafez, groaning. "They're on the bed, help yourself."

Uncle Mustapha went up to the bed, took a cigarette and lit it. It was a very cheap tobacco, and Uncle Mustapha smoked it with weary distaste. He sighed and recalled the luxurious cigarettes he had smoked during his zenith.

"I beg you, stop sighing," said old Hafez. "Why should you be so unhappy? Haven't you everything you want?"

Old Hafez felt nothing but scorn for his brother Mustapha, who had squandered his part of their inheritance in a marriage with a disreputable woman. When, after the catastrophe, he had allowed Uncle Mustapha to come to the house, he had not made a gesture of brotherly pity. Rather, he had hoped to be able to humiliate him. Uncle Mustapha, not long before, had been extremely arrogant with old Hafez—the only one who had resisted him. He had never concealed the fact that he considered old Hafez a timorous bourgeois, miserly and mean. Old Hafez had never forgiven him for this insulting attitude. Now he avenged himself.

"I'd like to talk to you," said old Hafez.

Uncle Mustapha was sitting on the edge of the bed. He smoked his cigarette with a terribly unhappy air.

"I'm listening," he said.

"Well!" continued old Hafez. "You know about my decision to marry."

"A happy decision," said Uncle Mustapha. "It would be good to have a wife to take care of you. Allow me to congratulate you."

"You can congratulate me later. Right now I want you to tell the children not to meddle in this affair. I suppose you're not in league with them. That would really be shameless ingratitude."

"Me!" said. Uncle Mustapha. "On the contrary, I've undertaken you defence. But I can't do anything with Rafik. He's capable of killing me."

"That's ridiculous! You've let yourself be frightened by a child! Rafik's a bad boy, and that's all. But I'll teach him."

"You're right."

"I'm always right. In any case, I'll be married in spite of everything. I've told Haga Zohra to find me a young woman of a good family. There are plenty around here. I plan to marry as soon as possible."

Uncle Mustapha didn't answer. He knew his brother's obstinacy and, above all, he remembered the story of the goat. It was a characteristic example of old Rafez's bad faith and spirit of contradiction, One day when he was walking on his land with a cousin, old Hafez—who was then in his fiftieth year—stopped in the middle of a field and noticed a black form at the summit of a rise of ground. It was rather far away, and neither he nor his cousin could make it out clearly enough to say exactly what it was. "It's a goat," old Hafez said at once. "It's a kite," replied his cousin. Old Hafez told him he was blind and persisted in his own idea. After a minute, as they were arguing, the object of dispute flew up in the air and lost itself on the horizon. "You see, it was a kite," cried the cousin, triumphant. Old Hafez retorted, not the least disturbed; "It was a goat, even if it flew away." Before such aberration, the cousin went away, indignant, and stayed angry with old Hafez for a long time.

"And you, what do you think of the marriage?" asked old Hafez.

"It's an excellent idea!" said Uncle Mustapha. "Heavens, I envy you!"

He had become disarmingly humble, not dreaming, himself, of the transformation. To live in this house, he had undergone a sort of enchantment. He had never thought that one day his money would be exhausted; he had let it all go. He had lived, a long time after his ruin, expecting a miracle. He didn't want to believe he had no more money.

He was still awaiting the miracle, even though it was impossible that a miracle could arise in this sordid room, with the infirm old man seated in his rocking chair, wanting to be married. Uncle Mustapha looked at his brother and, for a moment, thought he was dreaming that all this rotten atmosphere was only a snare devised by sleep. Suddenly, he felt a burning at his fingers; the cigarette was entirely consumed. He put it out in the ashtray on the night table and sighed again, as if to impress himself with the reality of his misfortune.

Old Hafez sprawled in his armchair; he twirled his moustache pensively.

"You haven't told me about the children's newest plots."

"They haven't any new plots. Only Rafik has taken possession of the dining room. He stays on the sofa, waiting for Haga Zohra. I don't think he'll be able to keep it up long."

"Cursed boy! And Galal, what's he doing?"

"He doesn't do anything, he sleeps as always. He's put Rafik in charge of the whole affair; he relies on him. He's an astonishing boy."

"Why do you say that?"

"No reason. Only to see him sleeping like that all the time seems rather strange to me."

"There's nothing strange about it, believe me. What do you want him to do? At least he's peaceful, he doesn't bother anyone."

Old Hafez frowned; his children were a burden to him. He didn't know how to make them reasonable, without disturbing himself.

"You'll have to talk to Galal," he continued, "He's the eldest; his brothers will listen to him."

"Talk to Galal!" exclaimed Uncle Mustapha, astounded. "You don't know what you're saying. He only gets out of bed to eat, and not always then. Do you know what he dared ask me once? It's really shameful! He asked me to bring him the chamber pot, because he wanted to use it and didn't want to disturb himself. It's barbarous, and I don't like it. Speak to him yourself."

"This is insane! Tell him to come up and see me. I don't know what you're good for. It's unspeakable that you can't give me the least help when I need you."

"It's easy to see you aren't used to being around them. Those children are impossible. They want to drive me crazy."

"Never mind! A man like you, you should be able to exert a little authority!"

Uncle Mustapha felt the vengeful irony in these reproaches. He saw himself caught in a circle of vile atrocities. The unreal atmosphere, the unused furniture, all the shabby comfort revolted his soul. And this dangerous sleep that submerged everything, like a devastating flood. He looked at his brother, this stupid old man who was dreaming of marrying, his enormous hernia bursting through his nightgown between his spread legs. He was fascinated by the hernia. It reminded him of an old scene that had had the same grotesque fascination.

It had happened so long ago it was nearly lost in the folds of his memory. It had occurred in a bachelor apartment he had rented in the city. A woman had come to wash his linen each week in the bathroom. Uncle Mustapha couldn't remember her face—an expressionless face, the sort that left no trace in one's mind. She was always silent and did her work with a tired, resigned air. Uncle Mustapha had lived for a long time without thinking about her actual presence, as if she moved in a separate existence on the edge of a dream. Then, one day, he didn't know how, a terrible thing happened: he slept with her. This only happened once, and Uncle Mustapha didn't think of it again until, several months later, he noticed the woman's stomach had become huge. He was worried and asked her if he was responsible. At each visit, the woman's stomach grew with an agonizing and precise rhythm. She always kept her passive beast's attitude, never pronouncing a word. It finally became unbearable; Uncle

Mustapha grew sick. Each week he watched this lewd stomach, and each week it seemed more impossibly swollen. He would have gone mad if the woman hadn't disappeared one day and never come back.

He roused himself from his memories and asked his brother: "How's your hernia?"

"Thank God," replied old Hafez, "it's getting better."

"You have to learn to take care of it," said Uncle Mustapha "It could be a real nuisance."

Old Hafez put his hand between his legs and caressed the swelling as one caresses a child.

"Don't you find it smaller?"

"It's hardly visible anymore," said Uncle Mustapha.

He wanted to appease his brother; his situation as a parasite demanded that he be courteous. Old Hafez knew he was lying, but his lie was agreeable all the same.

"Is that true?' he asked.

"On my honor, it's true. I wouldn't fool you! A few days ago, it was frightening. But now you can scarcely see it."

"May God hear you! I wish it would go away entirely. Do you think it will be an obstacle to my marriage?"

"How silly! Your wife will be happy to take care of you. I tell you, she'll even be proud of your hernia."

Old Hafez smiled contentedly. The enormity of this lie didn't seem to bother him. He lit a cigarette, offered another to his brother, and they began to smoke in silence.

VIII

Hoda was in no hurry to go back to her mother's; this evening she wanted to see Imtissal. Ever since Rafik had sent
her there, Hoda had been on friendly terms with the prostitute. She loved, most of all, to play with Imtissal's baby, and to
rock it on her knees while it slept. It was a beautiful child and
aroused Hoda's maternal instincts. The prostitute was always
very friendly; she spoiled Hoda, giving her syrups and all kinds
of sweets. Hoda didn't quite realize what it meant that Imtissal
was a prostitute. She had a rather confused idea about it, and it
didn't disturb her relationship with Imtissal. To her she could
talk about Serag, because the prostitute always listened with a
tender friendliness. Now there was a sort of conspiracy between
them. Hoda had no one else to whom she could tell her griev-
ances, and old Hafez's latest caprice, along with the whole load
of his contrariness and surprises, was too heavy for her to bear
alone. She wanted to tell Imtissal about this sensational event. It
would do her good to lighten her heart a little.

The night was long in coming, and in the grey twilight the

street lamps flickered weakly, like half-formed stars. Some people were lagging along the road, before going home to bed. The houses were already becoming black and immobile. In some places, there were long vistas over the fields; the country slept in its snare, and an infinite sadness stretched as far as the horizon. Hoda walked purposefully, with the bearing of a serious and well-bred young lady. She wore a blue beret and carried a large shoulder bag that knocked against her hip.

This bag was the height of elegance, a present from Imtissal, and Hoda was proud to show it off. Basically, she was given to coquetry, like the rest of her sex. She practised it with amusing naiveté. Imtissal lived at the end of the crowded area; after her house there were only a few villas scattered along the road. Hoda was frightened crossing the last yards that still lay between. She was seized by a superstitious terror. She almost ran, stopped in front of the house, panting, and raised her bead. There was a light in Imtissal's window. Hoda went in and climbed up the dark stairway with the worn steps. The bannister was rickety, and there were obscure designs on the wall. Hoda stopped on the second floor; Imtissal's door was on the right. She straightened her beret, smoothed her dress, licked her lower lip, then knocked on the door.

After a moment the door opened, and Imtissal appeared, her hair loose, her long body undressed for the night.

"It's you! Come in, darling!"

"I've come for a visit. Am I disturbing you?"

"On the contrary. I'm very happy to see you. Come in and sit down."

Hoda went into the room; she didn't sit down, but asked:

"Is the baby asleep?"

"Yes, but you can take him on your lap."

Hoda went over to the corner of the room where Imtissal kept the cradle; the child was sleeping. She took it gently in her arms, then sat on the ground and held the infant in her lap. She was overcome with joy.

Imtissal, the students' friend, sat negligently on the edge of the bed. She wore a yellow dressing gown, embroidered with large scarlet flowers. It revealed her full body that had an almost primitive sensuality. In the light of the kerosene lamp, her outrageously painted face looked like a mask. She had a heavy, tragic beauty.

"Tell me," she said. "Has Rafik sent you?"

"No, by Allah!" said Hoda. "I came by myself. I like to see you and play with the baby."

"I like to see you too."

"You're so nice to me."

"Aren't they nice to you?"

"They're terrible. The nicest one is Serag."

"That's because you love him," said Imtissal.

"I guess you're right," said Hoda.

"And does he love you?"

"I don't know. You can't ever tell with him."

"No one can ever tell with any of them," said Imtissal.

Her voice was husky and slow; it promised infinite sorrows and joys. She heaved a sigh and was silent. Since her experience with Rafik, she had nourished an unspeakable hatred for his family. She had never forgiven them for destroying her love, nor, especially, her dream of a more dignified life. Imtissal believed old Hafez had taken his son from her because she was a prostitute; she didn't understand the true reasons for his refusal. She had cursed him unto the tenth generation.

"They sleep all the time, don't they?" she asked.

"They did sleep," said Hoda. "But now they've all gone completely mad."

"Why, what's happened?"

"They're threatened by a real catastrophe."

"A catastrophe! What is it, darling?"

"It's my master. Can you believe it, he wants to get married!" said Hoda.

Imtissal burst into hysterical laughter; it shook her entire body.

"Oh, that's wonderful!" she said. "So old Hafez wants to get married! What does Rafik think of that?"

"He's the most upset of all. He swears all day long. He hardly sleeps anymore; he's waiting."

"What for?"

"He's waiting for Haga Zohra, the go-between. He wants to keep her from seeing my master. She's the one who's arranging the marriage."

Imtissal seemed to be overcome by a frantic gaiety. Her eyes shone; she clapped her hands and turned over on the bed.

"It's marvelous," she said. "Then they're awake and waiting. You can't imagine how this delights me. I'd love to see them!"

"It's not very amusing for me," said Hoda. "The whole load falls on me."

"I feel sorry for you, darling," said Imtissal. "I forgot you have to bear with all their extravagances."

She took the comb from the night table and began to comb her hair. She had black hair, very long, that hung all the way down her back, divided into two heavy plaits. Imtissal took great care of it. She knew the power of its secret aroma to arouse desire in the inexpert bodies of her young clients. She was a prostitute endowed with an exceptional temperament. Her business didn't tire her too much; above all, it wasn't repugnant to her. She felt no revulsion from her contact with her young lovers. Their ignorance and timidity in their search for pleasure amused her. She had taught many of them how to make love. She was proud and maternally concerned with their progress. Rafik was the only man she had ever loved. To him she had revealed the passionate secret of her body and all the experience acquired in her business. She had believed he would always love her; thus her deception was slow to heal. Then the baby had come.

The child slept on Hoda's knees, his pale face lined by the reflections of the lamp. She looked at it with a bitter smile on her painted mouth. She was afraid of seeing him grow; then she wouldn't be able to keep him in the room with her. Sometimes, when he cried, she had to hold him in her arms, while she submitted to a client's lovemaking. One day they would have to separate, or go elsewhere and live in larger quarters. This was her sole preoccupation now.

"Are you expecting anyone?" asked Hoda. "Tell me if I should leave."

"No. I'm not expecting anyone for the moment," said Imtissal. "You can stay. Go on."

"What more is there to say?"

"Tell me about Serag. Is he upset about his father's marriage?"

"Oh no! Serag only thinks of leaving to look for work. I'm afraid for him."

"Why are you afraid?"

"I don't know. Do you think they're made for work?"

"I think they're incapable of it. There's no danger of losing him. He'll give up the idea soon."

"May God hear you!" said Hoda. "It's given me a heavy heart."

"Yes," said Imtissal. "I know them, I know what they can do. They scorn people who work. They'd rather wet their pants than unbutton their trousers—it's too tiring."

"That's Galal," said Hoda. "He's exactly like that."

"That one I don't know," said Imtissal. "I've never seen him. When I came to live here, he was already buried in sleep. He seems to be their teacher. Rafik admired him tremendously."

"He's astonishing," said Hoda. "When I watch him, all at once I want to go to sleep myself."

Instinctively, at the memory of Galal, she opened her mouth and yawned. The child was heavy on her knees. She was tired from her day's work and her limbs felt stiff. The odor of the kerosene lamp, mingled with the aroma of perfume and cosmetics, was strange and heavy in the room. Hoda felt herself falling asleep. The great bed, the mirrored chest which reflected all Imtissal's movements, all the atmosphere of faded, cheap luxury, began to dizzy her. She saw Imtissal's supple, adorned body languishing on the rose quilt. One of her legs, slipping through her dressing gown, seemed, in the weak lamp light, like the supreme indecency of all flesh. Hoda felt drugged in the stagnant air; she heard the death-rattle of love infiltrate the silence. The room seemed, for the first time, strange and corrupting. She shook herself, blinked her eyes, and asked in a smothered voice:

"You don't want to see him again?"

"Who are you talking about?"

"I'm talking about Rafik," said Hoda. "He still devils me about you. He thinks it's my fault you won't see him."

"Tell him I'll never see him again," cried Imtissal. "And that I curse him with all my soul. To think he stuffs himself there, in the middle of his disgusting family. Ah! You don't know his pride! He's bursting with vanity. Do you know what he said to me one day, when he saw a funeral go by? That he wished he was the dead man. Because of the pomp of the cortege, you understand! How can anyone be so vain!"

"He told me he wanted to explain some things to you," said Hoda.

"What has he to explain? I don't want a single explanation. It's enough to know he's plunged in unhappiness! Ah! It's going to be so funny! I hope someone will pass out sugarplums at that rotten old man's wedding. Don't forget to bring me my share."

Imtissal had risen; she was standing now at the foot of the bed, in a martyred pose. A bitter pain twisted her highly painted face. Now she finally had her revenge! She bared her breasts and burst out in hysterical laughter.

★　★　★

The monotonous, insidious call of the corn vendor harassed him.

"Roasted corn! Eat some roasted corn!"

These wandering vendors—he despised them more than anything in the world; they cried their merchandise in the ears of the passers-by as if they offered an obscene invitation. This one was even worse than the others. He gave himself the airs of a conscientious, organized worker. The imbecile! He thought he was working because he pulled some ears of roasted corn on a cart! What stupidity! Rafik heard his call again, distorted by the distance, filling the night. He felt the mute cries of men around him, ready to devour him. He hurried on. The road was deserted now, but he felt the certain presence of monsters, always ready for murder. He felt them waiting behind the walls of houses, couching in the shadowy underbrush of the fields, and even in the dull sky above him.

Rafik prowled a few minutes under Imtissal's window. He didn't dare go up; he was afraid she'd be with a client. He'd never be able to survive such a humiliation! He suffered a deadly jealousy at the thought of Imtissal making love. He was tormented by visions; he stiffened under the intensity of his carnal memories. He glanced toward the entrance and was terrified by its look of a shadowy trap. The house was in deep shadow; the street lamps didn't penetrate it. Its sinister façade and crumbling walls seemed buried in the night. Rafik couldn't take his eyes off the entrance. His need to explain to Imtissal, that had brought him this far, had changed to a physical desire. Suddenly he felt himself torn apart, and a light split the darkness. A car passed at top speed, creating a wind of panic. Rafik felt himself caught and staggered like a drunken man. He couldn't stand the least shock. His head ached, his limbs were weak and painful; he was afraid of falling on the road.

The café he entered was a sort of dirty hovel, lit by a gas lamp. Some shaky tables swam in the weird light. The proprietor stood behind the counter. He was about thirty, with a dull face, and had a bird tattooed on his right temple. He was busily preparing a multitude of apparently useless things, since there was no one in the café, except a shriveled old woman, whose head was covered by a black veil. She was sitting near the counter and never took her troubled look off the man.

Rafik ordered a cup of coffee; he waited, half conscious, for his strength to return. He was angry with himself for his cowardice. He had gone out with the intention of seeing Imtissal, and he hadn't dared go up to her room.

Why hadn't he dared? His desire for her had stopped him. In leaving the house that evening, his mind had been free of all mental reservations; he had simply wanted to explain himself to her. It was only when he stood under her window, thinking that perhaps she was entertaining a client, that he had felt the blood rush in his veins. His desire for her was not yet dead. She had been too close to him, the warmth of her body was still alive in him. He felt caught in the memory of former voluptuousness.

At this moment he noticed a strange scene.

The café owner was talking to the old woman at the table near the counter. There was nothing remarkable in that; he spoke with his usual voice and gestures. Then, suddenly, he changed his voice and his movements, as though he were imitating someone else. For some time he alternated roles. First he was himself, then another person. This other person was always the same; he had a well-defined voice and manner. He could be recognized quickly as soon as he entered the scene. It seemed to unroll according to established rite; no false note interrupted its charm.

Rafik was intrigued by this mystery. He was also growing impatient for his coffee. He tapped on the table and caught the man's attention. The man nodded his head to show he had understood.

A moment later, he brought him his coffee. Rafik looked at the man curiously.

"Yes," said the man. "That's how it is!"

"What's that?" asked Rafik.

The man put a finger to his lips and leaned forward.

"That woman is my mother," he said.

"So?" said Rafik.

"She's mad," said the man.

"I see," said Rafik. "But what sort of comedy are you playing?"

"It's not a comedy," said the man. "Listen, here's the story. I had a brother who died last year. My mother doesn't believe it. She's crazy, I tell you. Well, so as not to distress her, I take my brother's gestures and voice. That way she thinks he's still alive, and that she sees him."

"What a story!" said Rafik.

"Yes, it's a pretty story!" said the man. "All this tires me enormously, especially with the work I do. Each time she comes here I have to begin these grimaces all over again."

"I pity you," said Rafik.

"It does me good to talk to someone," said the man. "You don't know what a burden all this is to me."

Rafik got up and left the café. He was upset by what he had

just seen. The collective insanity of mankind had never aston-ished him more. He knew its many forms. The café proprietor was as mad as his old mother! They were all mad. There was no salvation anywhere in the world. Rafik ran almost all the way back to the house.

IX

Now the mouse was under the bed; Galal heard it nibbling the strips of the parquet floor. He didn't dare move; he didn't even dare open his eyes. Sweat chilled his body, he felt it running in small rivulets along his limbs. Every evening this mouse came to destroy his sleep. It was obstinate; it turned round and round, then began to run from one end of the room to the other, making a tiny noise, scarcely perceptible. Galal had the disagreeable impression that it was running across his skin.

He lowered the covers and looked over at the other bed; Rafik wasn't there. Where could he be? They were all becoming maniacs in this house! What could keep them up like this, lost in their useless debates, as if they were plotting the end of the world? The idea made him smile. What if it really were the end of the world! A light flashed through his mind his father's marriage. It was true his father had decided to marry. And he'd slept for days, without worrying about anything! How was such a disaster possible? It would be unbearable! He must do everything he could to stop this marriage. He must act quickly. Act! The very thought sent painful cramps through his body.

Thus his sleep was menaced! Why hadn't he guessed the tragedy hidden in this marriage at once! A woman coming into a house would ruin a state of sleep established for an eternity. Once again he thought he would have to do something about this calamity. The best thing would be for his father to die. But this idea didn't attract Galal much. His father's death would bring complications of another order, just as disagreeable, if not more immediate. First, there would be the mourners who never failed to assemble. The cries of those infernal females would fill the house for days. And then, he would have to get up, to receive their condolences and follow the cortege to the cemetery.

No, it would be better if his father didn't die. He would have to find something else. Galal realized that the idea of the marriage was going to be an endless torment. He believed he was in great danger and didn't know what to do about it. No one was there to help him. Rafik was busy with the affair. That's why he wasn't in bed. Ah! Good boy! Perhaps he was murdering Haga Zohra! Galal had faith in him; he was almost an engineer, he had lots of profound technical knowledge. Galal felt a little calmer, but he still couldn't sleep.

What time could it be? In any case, it still wasn't dawn. Galal didn't remember having heard the carts go by. The carts came from a nearby factory, and took red bricks to the city. They passed on the road regularly, with a thunderous noise that shook the house to its foundations. Galal was awakened each time as though by an earthquake. He couldn't help thinking of the men who drove the carts. Agonized, he always asked himself what stupid miracle had awakened these men at dawn and sent them to work. It was something Galal could never understand.

The mouse seemed to be seized by a sudden frenzy; it leaped all over the room as though in search of some way out. Galal listened to it, scarcely breathing, the covers drawn up to his chin. Above all he feared it would jump into the bed. The thought drove him mad. He would have liked to have turned on the light, but to reach the switch he would have to make a crippling effort. He lay still under the blankets, forcing himself to forget everything, and tried to fall asleep again.

He felt some presence near him and started up.

"It's you!"

Uncle Mustapha was standing near the bed. He was dressed as usual and wore his tarboosh on his head.

"Are you going out?" asked Galal.

"No, I'm not going out," said Uncle Mustapha. "I'm worried."

"I see," said Galal. "You're always dressed as though you were going out. And that tarboosh! How can you stand it on your head? Isn't it heavy?"

"That doesn't matter," said Uncle Mustapha. "I beg you, wake up a minute."

"Say what you have to say," said Galal. "I'm awake. What do you want?"

"I'm worried," said Uncle Mustapha.

"Why? What's the matter now?"

"It's your brother, Rafik," said Uncle Mustapha. "He went out last evening and he isn't back yet."

Uncle Mustapha was silent and watched Galal. The night bulb in the hall sent a thin streak of light through the open door. In this, single beam, Galal's face seemed hideously pale, like that of a cadaver. Uncle Mustapha recoiled, appalled. He sat on Rafik's empty bed and sighed several times, even more profoundly than usual.

"You're worried for nothing" said Galal. "What time is it?"

"It's ten o'clock," said Uncle Mustapha.

"Is that all!" said Galal. "I thought it was much later."

"What bothers me," said Uncle Mustapha, "is that he doesn't usually go out. I don't understand it."

"Maybe Serag took him along to look for work," said Galal.

"That's impossible," said Uncle Mustapha. "Rafik wouldn't do it. He's never looked for work. Besides, Serag is in his room."

Actually, Uncle Mustapha's distress was only a pretext for coming to talk to Galal. He needed to talk to someone. He was growing feeble in this house; the deathlike silence oppressed his soul. His conscience also tormented him. The image of the washerwoman's swollen stomach wouldn't leave him. Ever since he had thought of her, he couldn't manage to get her out of his mind. Every day it grew more overwhelming. Uncle Mustapha couldn't fight it; the stomach swelling with mysterious life was crushing down on him, almost suffocating him. A strange thing was happening to him: he had begun to think about the child. What had become of it? Uncle Mustapha was ready to give some remorse to these reflections. His life was thus given a fixed point; he found this a charming relief. He could spend his leisure hours plumbing the remorse of his conscience. He finally felt like a man again!

"Then you've no idea where he could be?"

"Uncle Mustapha, I haven't any ideas. Don't you know that, or are you doing this on purpose? I'm very patient. But I want to be left alone."

"Don't be angry, my boy!"

"There's that cursed mouse too. That's why I was awake."

"Is there a mouse in this room?"

"Yes, it's over there chewing on God knows what!"

Uncle Mustapha had instinctively stiffened and drawn up his legs. He looked fearfully at the floor.

"I'll tell Hoda to set a trap," he said.

"Never mind," said Galal. "I don't want a trap. I might catch my foot in it."

There was a silence. Uncle Mustapha tried to hear the mouse. He stared at the line of light that came through the door; it was his only safeguard against the danger. But there was no noise. He raised his eyes and looked at Galal. In the half light, he saw his almost unreal face lit by an evil smile. He heard a faint snickering.

"Uncle Mustapha! I know where Rafik went!"

"Where, my boy?"

"He's undoubtedly gone to murder Haga Zohra! He's full of courage. He wants to rid us of our great misfortune!"

"Be quiet, Galal, my boy! You astonish me. You're a wise, thoughtful lad. And here you fling yourself beyond all reason!"

"The thing that's beyond all reason is this marriage."

"Your father wants to marry. It's his right. No one can stop him."

"What about our rights! Uncle Mustapha, haven't we the right to sleep in peace'?"

"What stops you from sleeping?"

"Uncle Mustapha, why do you play the fool? A child would understand. How can we sleep with a woman in the house? A woman who runs in and out all day, arranging everything around her. She'll want everything right and proper to impress the neighbors. She'll begin by getting a maid, because little Hoda won't be enough for her. Imagine it, Uncle Mustapha, a maid in the house! It makes me tremble! Without counting all her relatives! They'll come visit us. We'll have to get up and dress to meet them. We might even have to talk to them. What kind of life would that be, I ask you!"

"You're exaggerating, my boy! And then, your father wants it. He's the master. After all, he wouldn't be so disagreeable if there was a woman in the house. Life would be much pleasanter."

Uncle Mustapha had built a delightful picture of the change his brother's marriage might make in the life of the house. He already rejoiced at the thought of receiving people, and perhaps, even, of paying visits.

"Uncle Mustapha, I always thought you were a traitor. But not that way! You must want to see us all dead!"

"Calm yourself! I haven't said anything so tragic, believe me!"

"Let me sleep. Who knows if our days for sleeping aren't numbered already! I don't want to talk anymore."

"I beg you, don't go back to sleep. Talk to me a little longer."

Uncle Mustapha didn't want to go back to his room. The image of the washerwoman's swollen stomach was up there, waiting for him. This evening he didn't feel strong enough to face it. It was like a tatter of living flesh that he could only touch with infinite caution. He wanted to rest, as long as he could, in this shadowy corner, face to face with a human being, even if he was half buried in sleep.

"Listen to me! Maybe the marriage will never take place."

Galal rose up in the bed, just enough to show his astonishment.

"Why not?"

"Because of the hernia!"

"What hernia?"

"Your father's hernia, you'll see!"

"My father has a hernia?"

"You didn't know?"

"No. How should I know? That's extraordinary news. I knew he had diabetes. I even thought it was a lucky thing and would make it easier for him to marry."

"Not at all. The diabetes was Haga Zohra's idea. The truth is your father has a hernia."

"Have you seen it?"

"As I see you now. It's enormous!"

There was a solemn silence.

"Then we're saved!" cried Galal.

"I think so," said Uncle Mustapha.

"Well! Uncle Mustapha, thank you for the news. You can go now. I'll be able to sleep."

Uncle Mustapha got up in spite of himself yet he still hesitated to leave. But he already heard Galal snoring and knew it was useless to insist. He left the room with the sad face of an abandoned man.

★ ★ ★

The sudden glare of the electric lamp fell on him like cold water. He gave a start and sat up in the bed.

"You must be crazy to turn on the light without even warning me."

"Excuse me, I couldn't find my pajamas."

It was Rafik who had just come in and was undressing nervously.

"Well, did you kill her?"

"Kill who?"

"Good heavens, have you forgotten? Weren't you supposed to kill Haga Zohra? What a fool I was to count on you."

"I haven't forgotten a thing. Don't do anything, I'll kill her one day."

"Where were you? Uncle Mustapha was worried about you. He was in here bothering me about it."

Galal kept his eyes shut while he talked; he couldn't bear the hard glare of the electric light. He seemed like a blind man, his hands twitching in the void.

"Turn off that light, I beg you!"

Rafik had finished undressing and tied his pajamas. He turned out the light and lay down on his bed. He seemed determined to sleep.

Galal's voice rose in the darkness:

"Listen: Uncle Mustapha just gave me some wonderful news."

"What news?" asked Rafik.

"It's news of the greatest importance for all of us," said Galal feverishly. "Father has a hernia."

Rafik stirred, then leaned over the bed.

"You're sure Uncle Mustapha wasn't lying?"

"I don't think so. He told me he'd seen it. The marriage won't take place."

"It's a good thing," said Rafik in a dreamy voice. "Is it big?"

"It seems that it's enormous! We can relax."

"Not entirely," said Rafik. "I'll still have to wait for Haga Zohra. She's a damned good go-between. She could marry off a corpse."

They slept with peace in their souls, thinking of their father's hernia that had saved them from disaster.

X

Standing on the embankment, Serag inspected his surroundings and found himself at the same spot where he had seen the child hunting with a slingshot. He was certain he would soon appear again from behind the tall stalks of corn. The sycamore stood before him at the side of the path, and he heard birds twittering in its branches. The path wound across the corn field and the road was at the end, lost in vaporous distance. Serag trembled at the slightest noise, looking around with a lost air. He was sad because the child wasn't there. In going out that morning to look at the unfinished factory, Serag had thought of him, telling himself he must wander around this neighborhood. He was disappointed not to see him. He had imagined the child would have to be there, waiting, and he was almost angry with him for this betrayal.

He looked around again, but saw no trace of the child. He didn't know what to do now. The child's absence was a bad sign. Fate was against him. He had intended to go to the city with him. He wanted to link himself to the child, and follow him to exciting adventures. But the child had deserted him; he traveled the roads alone, fearless. Serag thought he would never find him again. He felt a bitter nostalgia at the memory of their first meeting.

He was tired from having waited in vain for the child. He still had to go as far as the factory; his supreme hope lay there. He came down from the embankment and started across the fields.

It was almost summer now. It was a hot day and Serag was uncomfortable in his heavy sweater. He thought he would have to change his outfit if he kept up these visits. Perhaps he would even have to buy some dark glasses to protect his eyes from the sun. Nevertheless, this heat was better than the changeable winter weather. There was no chance of wind or rain. There were no more heavy, sullen clouds, bringing sadness and desolation. Serag felt the desire for adventure stronger than ever. New blood seemed to be moving in his veins. Life with his family had become unbearable. Ever since his father had decided to marry, a demon seemed to have come into the house. Rafik was up in arms; even Galal no longer slept as much as usual. It was really pitiful to see Galal so upset; he had become almost human. Serag suffered for him.

He routed these harassing thoughts and walked faster. This brightness all around opened unsuspected horizons. He imagined he was really going to work. It was a beautiful illusion and Serag smiled contentedly.

He reached the top of the little hill, puffing. Now he could see the factory; it looked the same as it had on his last visit—no change in its half finished walls—the same sad abandonment, the same hostile air. Serag saw a man crouched near a hut. In front of him was a little wood fire on which he was cooking his meal. Serag felt a ray of hope, but he quickly saw that the man was a caretaker and not a worker. He wondered for a moment if he should ask him about the factory. Then he would finally know why it wasn't finished, and if it would ever be finished. The man should know. However, Serag hesitated about making the extra walk. He was still rather far from the man, and the way was uneven and full of obstacles. It was really a rather hazardous walk. But Serag dearly wanted to know what chance he had of working in the factory. This was his only hope of finding out. He gathered his courage, walked down the hill, and, gritting his teeth, began to cross the cluttered ground towards the walls of the factory.

He moved with difficulty among the piles of huge rocks that lay scattered in the sun. The ruts impeded his steps. It was even more dangerous than he'd imagined. Several times he almost fell. He seemed to be going down an endless road. Finally, he stopped. It was the first time he had ever seen a factory so close. He was frightened by these walls that seemed to conceal the desperate labour of men. He saw them grow before him as if to rebuff his sacrilegious presence.

Serag stepped over a pile of old iron and found himself standing in front of the man. He looked at him for a moment in silence.

"Hello!

The man raised his head and replied in an indifferent tone:

"Hello!"

He was cooking beans on his wood fire. He was very old, his clothes patched like a beggar's rags. A long heavy stick was lying near him on the ground.

"Are you the caretaker?" asked Serag.

"Yes," said the man. "What do you want?"

"Excuse me," said Serag. "But I'd like to know why they don't finish this factory."

"Allah alone can say," said the man. "I was told to stay here; that's all I know."

They didn't speak for a moment. The man took no notice of anything but his beans. He turned them with a piece of iron like a spoon. Now and then he inhaled the aroma and closed his eyes in satisfaction. Serag watched him, irritated and impatient. He wouldn't learn anything after all!

"Then you don't know anything?"

"Why does it interest you?" asked the man. "Leave the factory alone!"

'Oh well!" said Serag, "I thought I might be able to work here."

"You're looking for work?" asked the man.

He looked at Serag, perplexed, scrutinizing him from head to toe and shaking his head.

'You don't look like a workman," he began. "An effendi like you doesn't work in a factory."

"That's no reason," said Serag. "I can work very well. I've already been here several times; I could do a lot of things."

He was terribly tired. But he forced himself to assume an easy, friendly manner. He wanted the caretaker's good opinion. He imagined that perhaps he could recommend him to the director of the factory.

"No, my son. It's no work for you."

The beans were cooked; the man took them off the fire. Before beginning to eat, he said politely:

"Help yourself."

"Thank you," said Serag. "I'm not hungry."

He sat on a large rock, facing the man. The sun burned over the whole countryside; it was almost noon. Serag was hot and thirsty.

"Have you been here long?"

"A few months," said the man. "But I won't stay much longer. It's hard work. I have to watch over these stones and piles of iron all the time. There are bandits who come to steal everything. And I'm responsible for it, you understand!"

"It's very important work," said Serag.

"Extremely important," said the man. "And I'm the only one who does it. There should be at least forty people to guard all this!"

Serag had a sudden inspiration. He could help the old man! That would always be a job, while he waited for them to finish the factory.

"Really, do you need help?"

"Of course I do," said the man. "At least forty people."

"I'd like to work with you very much," said Serag. "What do you say?"

"You want to be a watchman?"

"Yes, I could help you guard these stones."

"My word, you're a strange boy! What would your mother say?"

"My mother's dead. She wouldn't say anything."

"Even so, I can't. It's no work for you."

"I beg you, say yes! I want to work so much!"

"Why, do they beat you at home?"

"No one beats me," said Serag. "I want to go away. I've decided to work."

"You'll make your parents weep," said the man. "This will be black news for them."

The man stopped eating; he appeared to be reflecting. This boy seemed very peculiar to him. He began to suspect he had criminal intentions. Perhaps he was a thief. He wanted information so he could come back at night with his accomplices.

Serag was full of hope as he waited for the man's decision.

"Don't you want me?"

"No, I don't want you," said the man in a menacing voice. "And I advise you to leave quickly."

Serag was alarmed; he didn't understand.

"Why are you angry? Pardon me if I've bothered you!"

"Yes, you bother me. Get along and don't come back. Or I'll call the police!"

"The police!" said Serag, choking.

"I'll call the police!" the man repeated.

He seized his long stick, and looked as though he might use it. He had become evil-tempered. He slobbered and some bits of chewed food rolled on to his beard. Serag hesitated a second, then left as fast as he could, without looking back.

It was over now. He would never work in the factory. His last chance had failed him. This incident with the old man had ended his illusions. He wouldn't even be able to come look at his dream. Life would become completely monotonous and insipid without this ideal that had sustained him in his worst moments. Serag felt completely discouraged. The factory had played a prominent role in his life; he had thought of it every day, and now, suddenly, he felt lost; he no longer had a pretext to justify his inaction. From now on he wouldn't be able to deceive himself.

He had reached the road and walked with his head down, indifferent to the harsh cries of the street vendors who passed. Some servants were doing their marketing, talking in shrill voices. He passed Abou Zeid's shop without stopping; he was in no mood to hear his lamentations. Anyhow, Abou Zeid was sleeping, stretched out on the threshold of the shop, paying no attention to him. That was a blessing. Serag couldn't have endured a talk with the peanut vendor. He had no new ideas for him and felt guilty. A little farther on he recognized Hoda among a group of servants standing around a lettuce cart. The young girl saw him too, and came up to him, running. She was carrying a heavy bag of groceries.

"So this is when you do your marketing," said Serag. "You're going to be late with lunch."

"It isn't my fault," said Hoda. "The master was asleep, and I didn't have any money. I had to wait till he woke up."

"I'm very hungry," said Serag. "Go on back to the house, girl."

"I'll go back with you," said Hoda.

There was no way to get rid of her. Serag saw she was so happy he didn't dare send her away. Hoda beamed with joy. She took Serag's hand, and they walked along, hand in hand, like two lovers. Serag was embarrassed when people passed them, but he didn't draw his hand away. He even liked to be extravagant in front of these people who knew him. Hoda looked at him and smiled.

"I want to tell you something."

"What's that?"

"I was very proud this morning."

"Ah! What of, foolish!"

Hoda swallowed and said very seriously:

"Before I did the marketing, I walked down the road with Imtissal's baby. And do you know what people thought?"

"No."

"They thought it was my baby. They smiled at the baby and looked at me with admiration. I was so proud of it!"

"You're just a fool! What an idea! So that's how you spend your time when you should be taking care of the house."

"I'm not a fool. I've grown up. You're the one who doesn't understand anything."

She let go of Serag's hand and walked alone, pouting.

XI

"You're going away and leave me all alone!" said Hoda.

"Yes. I'm going to the city. I can't stay in this house any longer."

That morning, Serag had resolved to leave for the city. Since he had lost the hope of working at the factory, there had been an immense void in his life. He had to fill that void. His visits to the unfinished factory had made him feel he was performing heroic deeds; he had drawn a certain moral strength from them. But now that this chimera had vanished completely, he found himself drawn toward sleep. He couldn't resist it anymore. Fatally, he was letting himself be overcome by an inexorable idleness. His family's listlessness was poisoning him more every day. Thus he had decided to leave as soon as possible. A few more days and he wouldn't have the strength to try.

"You won't do it," said Hoda. "You'll make me so unhappy!"

"Be quiet, foolish! Go do your work!"

"Where are you going? By Allah, you'll get lost!"

"It's none of your business."

He was standing near the window, trying to be stern. He felt this obstinate girl would weaken him; love was even worse than sleep. It was going to be harder than he had realized. He shouldn't have said anything to her. Now she would arouse the whole house.

He heard her whimpering and turned around.

"Now don't start crying!"

She wiped her eyes and came up to him, her hands out, imploring him.

"Stay here! Don't go away!"

"Be quiet, you daughter of a whore! They'll hear you and come to devil me too. I'm sorry I told you I was leaving."

"Then take me with you."

"You're mad! I'm not going to load myself down with a girl like you. I have to look for work."

"You can't work. I know you. I'll work for you!"

"Don't be stupid! I'd do anything to leave this house."

She realized he had really decided to go, and was panic stricken. How could she stop him from leaving? She only knew the temptations of the flesh. A faint hope rose in her. Her smile was malicious.

"If you leave, you won't be able to make love to me."

"I don't want to. Who told you I wanted to make love to you? I've other things to do, can't you understand?"

"That's not true!"

She pressed against him, trying to excite him. But he seemed weary and distant; he pushed her away brutally.

"Get out! Leave me alone!"

Hoda fell on the bed, a little stunned by the blow. But she wasn't through; she was ready to do anything to hold him. Scarcely moving her hand, she raised her dress, completely uncovering her thighs. She spread her legs and waited. The silence was agonizing. She saw him looking at her with a distant, tired stare. She trembled with fear and passion.

"You don't want me?"

He seemed out of his head; he didn't understand what she meant. He murmured in a desperate voice:

"No, I don't want you. I want to leave."

She pulled down her dress and got up. She was furious and ready to cry again.

"No one will keep me from going!"

Serag watched her leave the room, disturbed. She would tell them now; they would come preach to him. He began to dress hurriedly. He meant to resist their advice and their cowardly temptations.

Rafik was the first to appear.

"What's the matter! Are you leaving?"

"Yes, I've decided to look for work in the city."

Rafik was astounded; he'd just woken up. His mind was confused and he couldn't deal with such a serious situation. It was very difficult. Finally, he said:

"Have you any money?"

"What for?"

"You're going to the city without any money?"

"I'm going to work, I tell you. I'll earn money."

"Poor boy! Do you think they're just waiting to make you a minister?"

"I don't want to be a minister! What makes you think I do?"

"Then what do you want to be?"

"I don't know. I beg you, leave me alone. I have to think about what to take."

Rafik sat down on the bed, pondering the gravity of the case. He feared the worst for his brother. This idea of looking for work in the city was a trap of the Devil. It would bring all sorts of complications, would utterly destroy the innermost recesses of their retreat. There'd be no end to watches and waiting. Now that the danger of his father's marriage was almost removed by the news of the hernia, Rafik was dismayed at this new threat to their sleep. It was a vicious circle; they would never get out of it.

"Listen," he said. "I've discovered a secret."

"What secret?" asked Serag.

"I don't think Father can marry after all," said Rafik. "We've had incredible luck!"

"That doesn't interest me," said Serag. "Why should I care whether or not Father marries!"

"O traitor," said Rafik. "Never mind! I just want you to know we're in no danger. We'll be able to sleep peacefully. Life will be pleasant again."

"But I don't want to sleep," cried Serag. Who told you I wanted to sleep?"

"No one," said Rafik. "But all men like to sleep. You're a monster! I'm not going to waste any more time on you."

"You've been wearing yourself out for nothing," said Serag. "I'm going. No one can stop me."

Rafik didn't answer; he looked as though he might fall asleep. He remained silent for a few moments, then opened his eyes and said:

"You're not afraid?"

"What would I be afraid of?"

"Of streetcars," said Rafik. "They're terrible. They crush thousands of people every day!"

"That's not true," said Serag. "You just have to watch out and not walk on the tracks."

"But can you watch out?" said Rafik.

"Why not? I'm not blind."

"You're worse than blind," said Rafik. "By Allah, you'll get lost on the way. You won't be able to get back to the house."

"I don't plan to come back," said Serag. "You'd better go back to bed. Hoard your energy to watch for Haga Zohra! Why worry about me?"

"I'm not worried about you, imbecile! I'm thinking about our peace. When you leave all kinds of talk will start. And I don't want it! Father's marriage is enough! We're trying to stop a scandal and you're already starting another. My God! You'll kill me!"

"Ah! That's what you're thinking about! I thought it was just your affection for me."

"You're an ass!"

Serag had finished dressing; he was tying up a bundle that held a few clothes. It was his baggage. He was proud of it; now he was sure of leaving.

At this moment, they heard a groaning in the hall, and old Hafez appeared in the doorway, supported by Uncle Mustapha, who seemed to be feeling his own importance.

"What do I hear? You want to leave!"

"Yes, Father."

"Where, ungrateful son?"

"I want to go to the city, Father!"

"To the city!" cried old Hafez. "You hear! He says he wants to go to the city. What have I done to God to be given such a son?"

Uncle Mustapha, his tarboosh quivering on his head, his voice authoritative, addressed Rafik:

"Move a little. Let your father sit down."

Rafik drew back against the wall and old Hafez sat down on the edge of the bed. He settled his hernia comfortably between his legs, breathed painfully and said:

"Now explain this to me. What is this madness?"

"It's not madness," said Serag. "Father, try to understand; I want to work."

"Allah help us! You want to work! Why? What don't you like about this house?"

"I can't tell you, Father! I need to go away."

"Ungrateful son! I've fed you and dressed you all these years and this is my thanks!"

"What ingratitude is there in wanting to work, Father? I don't understand."

"You want to cover us all with shame!"

Old Hafez was thinking of the ridicule Serag's departure would bring the family; he trembled for his marriage. Such a scandal would surely cost him the good will of respectable people. He already had worries enough because of his infirmity which, at least, wouldn't be seen until his wedding night. But if his youngest son left, and especially to go to work, he would really be overwhelmed by shame.

"Father, let me go! I promise to come back tonight. Don't worry."

"And who says you can come back! You think people can come and go as they please? What if the police arrest you?"

"Why would the police arrest me?" asked Serag, stunned.

"For nothing," said old Hafez. "Then there are the streetcars, the automobiles, the cabs—all kinds of dangers. And what about the government. You're not afraid of the government?"

"What's the government going to do?'

"The government's against revolts," said old Hafez. "They'll put you under arrest."

"But I haven't done anything against the government," said Serag.

"The government won't ask you for explanations. They'll lock you up, I tell you!"

"Because I want to work?"

"Yes, those are subversive ideas; can't you understand that? I'd like to know who put such ideas in your head. You were born in an honorable family. I beg you not to ruin our reputation."

"Especially right now when we need it," said Rafik.

Old Hafez seemed to ignore Rafik, lying behind him on the bed. He had caught the sarcasm in his words, but controlled himself, and gave vent to several menacing groans. He didn't want to make the scene any worse. His first concern was Serag's departure. He'd take care of Rafik later.

"Why are you awake! My word! It's only dawn!"

It was Galal, awakened by the noise of the discussion. He feared some new mishap and had come to find out what the trouble was.

"It's your brother Serag," said Rafik. "He's decided to go to the city to look for work."

"Poor boy!" said Galal. "God help him."

"God is with the lazy," said Rafik. "He has nothing to do with the vampires who work."

"You're right," said Galal. "Where can I sit down?"

He looked around, saw the bed occupied, and slid down against the wall. He put his head on his knees and went back to sleep.

"Good heavens, he's asleep!" said old Hafez. "Galal, wake up! Speak to your brother. You're the eldest, maybe he'll listen to you. He doesn't listen to me, his own father."

Galal raised his head wearily; he seemed irritated.

"You want me to talk to a fool! I've enough trouble with the mouse."

"The mouse!" said old Hafez. "He's dreaming. What can I do?"

"There's nothing to do," said Serag. "I have to go."

"You hear," said old Hafez. "He's going to leave. I have no control over this boy!"

"Let him go," said Rafik. "He'll learn about life. It will teach him a lesson."

He got up slowly, leaned over and looked between his father's legs. He wanted to see the hernia. The hernia was there, very noticeable under his nightgown. It was even bigger than he'd hoped. He smiled diabolically and lay down again.

"I'll buy you a new suit," said old Hafez, at the end of his arguments. "Does that please you? You can go to the tailor's today. What more could you ask for? You see, I do everything to be agreeable."

"It's not a new suit I want," moaned Serag. "Father, don't you ever understand?"

"How do you expect me to understand?" said old Hafez. "Ungrateful child! Do I go out? Do I go to the city? What makes you any better than me? By Allah, I'm sorry I sent you to school! What did they teach you at school, tell me?"

Uncle Mustapha hadn't said anything. He didn't dare speak for fear of giving himself away. Actually, he was the only one who appreciated this departure, who thrilled at this promise of adventure. He, too, wanted to go away, to leave the house and the sleep-filled disorder that was like a nightmare. He gazed at Serag, moved to tears. He would have liked to go with him.

"My dear Serag," he said, "if you ever go to the city, don't forget to go by Emad El Dine Street. That's where my apartment was."

"Your apartment," said old Hafez. "What has your apartment to do with this?"

"I'd like him to see it, that's all," said Uncle Mustapha.

"This is impossible," said old Hafez. "You're inciting the child to leave with such ideas. Is that how you help me?"

"He wants to show us he lived in a nice apartment," said Rafik. "Don't bother, we'll take you at your word."

"That's not what I meant, I assure you," said Uncle Mustapha.

"Drop this," said old Hafez. "Haven't you any pity for your old father?"

"You're making us unhappy," said Uncle Mustapha.

"I'm not trying to make you unhappy," said Serag. "I just want to work."

"How can we help being unhappy if we know you're working," said old Hafez. "We're not egoists like you. Come, be reasonable. You're going to make me weep."

Old Hafez began to sniffle very effectively. He had decided on this as a last recourse to soften his son. Uncle Mustapha joined him. He had been holding back his tears but now he could let them flow. They had reached the crisis of the drama. No one, after this, could do anything.

"All right," said Serag. "I won't go. Only, I beg you, stop crying."

"At last you're reasonable!" said old Hafez. "You're a joy to your father. Come kiss me!"

Serag went up to his father and kissed him on the forehead. He felt miserable and ashamed.

Old Hales began to call for Hoda in a piercing voice that woke Galal.

"What's the matter now? Where are we?"

"He's not going," said Rafik.

"So much the better," said Galal. "Then this is over. I can go back to bed."

Hoda was waiting anxiously in the kitchen for the result of this family debate. She came running at her master's call.

"Come here, girl!" said old Hafez. "You're to fix a chicken for lunch today. Do you hear?"

He turned to Serag and said:

"Serag, my son, don't worry. We'll all go see the city some day."

"Don't count on me," said Galal.

XII

There was nothing but those street lamps that flickered in the night, creating, all along the road, large patches of provocative shadow. Each time he reached one of these spaces in the night, Rafik slackened his pace and savored a moment of peace. He had really decided to see her; he didn't hesitate as he had the last time. The desire he had felt for her was gone, leaving no trace of regret or bitterness. He'd thrown it away as a dead thing. He realized now that this long forgotten desire of the flesh would inevitably have led to an end of his happiness. He no longer wanted anything but the endless joy of sleep.

He felt lighter, as though moved by a gentle, tranquil power that seemed to have taken possession of him. To have grasped this elemental truth, hidden at the bottom of life—the way of the least effort—filled him with pride and gratitude. He felt as though he were floating in a decaying world that hadn't yet discovered its true nature. The stupidity of men was boundless. Why did they have to struggle, always vicious and discontented, when the sole wisdom lay in a careless, passive attitude? It was so simple. The least beggar could have understood it!

When he thought of his fate if he had gone off with Imtissal, Rafik felt a shiver of terror. Today he would have been a slave among other slaves. And for a woman! Because she would have induced him to work—forced him to work with her inane stubbornness and female unscrupulousness.

It was this woman he was now going to see, to explain his past attitude and his real reason for having left her. He didn't want to let a misunderstanding based on a pitiful, unhappy love affair go on any longer. She must know the truth. Rafik became more elated as he came nearer Imtissal's house. This final explanation would relieve him of an enormous pressure that weighed upon his sleep. He must destroy this illusion of love and conclude it with dignity.

He was feeling more and more buoyant when he heard himself called. He straightened up, made a few hesitant steps then stopped. He turned, suspiciously.

"I've been calling you for ages," said Mimi. "Didn't you hear me?"

"No," said Rafik. "What is this! Are you following me now?"

"Oh no," said Mimi. "Believe me. I was just in the house, looking out the window. I saw you go by and ran after you."

Mimi was breathless and seemed a little out of his head. He wasn't wearing a jacket, and his shirt was open on his chest. His whole appearance betrayed his hurry, and, also, a delirious joy.

"Why did you run after me?' said Rafik in a hostile tone. "What do you want?"

"I wanted to talk to you," said Mimi, affecting a confidence that exasperated Rafik.

"Well talk! I'm listening."

"May I walk with you?" asked Mimi. "Just for a minute?"

Rafik hesitated, but the pleasure of humiliating Mimi was too strong. He knew the young man's passion for his respect, and he had a sudden desire to hurt him. He said, with an edge of malice in his voice:

"I'm glad to see you. Walk with me if you like."

"This is really good luck," said Mimi. "I was just thinking about you when you went by."

Mimi couldn't quite believe in this happy encounter, for he had dreamed of it for so long. He behaved like an awkward lover, showing off with absurd gestures, and smiling a wonder-struck smile. He hadn't detected the cold malice in Rafik's last words and already believed in his success. However, he felt he must act with great discretion, because Rafik, he knew, was always on guard. He mustn't offend him. While walking beside Rafik in the obscurity of the night, he looked at him constantly. He wanted to be sure of his entire willingness.

Rafik was walking with an indifferent air. He was aware of all the emotions his presence aroused in his companion, and secretly rejoiced at his uneasiness. He was waiting until he declared himself to deal him a crushing blow. But Mimi didn't seem to want to talk; happiness had made him mute.

Now they were crossing the lighted circle beneath a street lamp. Rafik suddenly felt he couldn't hold back his impatience any longer. He turned toward Mimi and asked:

"What did you want to talk to me about?"

Mimi faltered a moment. The brutality of this question had taken him unawares. He seemed to have forgotten everything, thinking only of the joy of being with Rafik. His smile disappeared, and he stammered;

"I wanted to ask you to come to my house and see my paintings. I must know what you think of them."

"Well, you've wasted your time!" said Rafik. "I'm not coming to see your pictures. Besides, I don't know anything about painting. My opinion wouldn't be any use to you!"

"That's not true," said Mimi. "I know your ability. You're the only intelligent person in the whole quarter. All the others are asses."

"What makes you say that?" said Rafik.

"I know your philosophy of life," said Mimi. "It's magnificent."

"It's astonishing that you know something about my philosophy of life," said Rafik. "I've never confided in you."

"I know," said Mimi. "But I've understood all alone. The whole quarter is always saying absurd things about you and your family. I always have to defend you."

"That's very amusing," said Rafik. "May I know what they say?"

"They say you're all idlers," said Mimi. "And that you've sunk to the depths of laziness. They also tell an extraordinary story. It really goes beyond the limits of imagination. I don't dare tell you. You'll think I'm an idiot."

"What story?" asked Rafik.

"Well!" said Mimi. "Forgive me, but they say your brother Galal sleeps for months at a time, and that it takes a pair of pliers to open his eyes."

"All that's perfectly true," said Rafik. "My brother Galal has been sleeping for seven years. He only wakes up to eat."

Mimi stopped and looked at Rafik. He suspected a joke, but Rafik's serious expression made him change his mind. Such a thing was possible then! He was stunned, unable to speak a word.

Rafik watched him fixedly and waited. It amused him to have aroused this state of foolish astonishment in Mimi. He didn't move for a moment, his face impassive; then he began to walk on into the night. Mimi followed him silently.

"Ah! I like that kind!"

"What kind?"

"Like your brother Galal. To sleep seven years! What an artist!"

"You think he's an artist?"

"Certainly. That's what I try to explain to the imbeciles in this quarter. They take you for idlers."

"But it's the truth. Why contradict them?"

"They're asses, I tell you. They don't understand the beauty there is in this idleness. You're an extraordinary family. And you, Rafik, you're the only intelligent man in the world."

"You think so?"

"I'm never wrong about you. And I've never understood why you've detested me. Don't you feel that the two of us could revolutionize this quarter?"

"Since you understand my philosophy of life, you should know that I don't like noise and that I'm too fond of my tranquility."

"I'm talking about a moral revolution. We could teach these fools, these married men, what real wisdom is. I, with my painting, I express nothingness. It's a shame you don't write. But it's true you're a living example. That's enough."

Mimi was becoming exalted in talking; he came closer and closer to Rafik, speaking almost into his ear. He did not suspect the trap Rafik was setting for him. He was too happy to discern the least malevolence in Rafik's affable conversation. His passion had blinded him; he let himself be seduced by his own words, ardently desiring that the road would grow longer and that the night would cover their idyll eternally. However, at moments, he sensed a subtle menace insinuating itself between him and his companion. It was a disagreeable sensation and Mimi forced himself to escape it by brushing against Rafik as if to prove his presence more strongly.

Rafik, disgusted, pulled away from Mimi, then turned on him with the sudden desire to leap at his throat. But he controlled himself; he didn't want to give his game away yet. He was still waiting for Mimi to go far enough to destroy him with one blow. There was still time to check him when he became bolder. To tell the truth, he didn't want to admit to himself that Mimi's philosophy of life had aroused his curiosity. He had forgotten his mission and thought no more of Imtissal. He asked:

"And how do you express nothingness?"

"I paint the canvas in one color," said Mimi. "Some of them are black, some red, some green. It depends on my mood. The important thing is that they represent nothing."

"In short it's nothing colored," said Rafik.

"Exactly," said Mimi, "You've understood me perfectly. I knew that you would. We're made to understand each other."

Mimi was ravished by this interest Rafik seemed to take in his painting. He thought he was living in a dream. Never had Rafik been so agreeable or so understanding. He forgot all his past injuries, walking with his eyes on the sky, smiling at the stars. He stumbled against a stone, almost fell and caught Rafik's arm. Rafik gave him a look full of hatred.

"I forbid you to touch me. I don't like your ways."

"Don't be angry. I didn't do it on purpose. Listen. You must know that no one has ever seen my canvases. You'll be the first to see them."

"Thank you for the honor."

"Oh! Don't thank me. It's a great joy for me. I can't wait to know what you think of them."

Rafik stopped, crossed his arms and looked hard at Mimi.

"It's no use. I'm not coining to see your canvases."

Mimi shook his head in astonishment.

"Why? What have I done? You were so nice just now."

"You really thought I was being nice?" sneered Rafik. "Well, my dear Mimi, you were a fool to believe it! I don't like your ways. You're a phony. You're not even an invert."

"Me?" said Mimi, mortally offended. "I'm not an invert? You don't know me. You don't know what I can do."

"I don't want to know," said Rafik.

He had just struck Mimi at the heart of his pride, and he was overjoyed. Now he was finished with him. He only had to get rid of him. He walked on, hurrying.

Mimi seemed to have collapsed. It was as though Rafik's words had struck him fatally. He remained without moving for a long time, standing by the side of the road. He hadn't expected this supreme insult. No injury could have wounded him so deeply as this denial of his abnormality. All his artistic vanity expressed itself in the display of his inversion. For Rafik to deny this! He couldn't bear it. Suddenly he realized he was alone and an overwhelming terror seized him. He began to run after Rafik, uttering loud cries. But he couldn't catch him.

XIII

She was weary now; all afternoon a gang of college students had played truant in her room. They did this often, at least twice a week. While their parents believed them away at school, they came to her room and gave themselves up to a kind of little orgy. They brought with them a bottle of whiskey and some cigarettes, made a lot of noise and caroused like madmen. Then they went stumbling away with dark circles under their eyes, overjoyed at believing themselves already men. Imtissal loved these riotous gatherings and the tender promiscuity of youth made bold and feverish by her nakedness. They made love by turns and behaved as if it were a question of sportive competition. Afterwards, each bragged before his comrades of his own prowess. The victor of the day was known all over the quarter, but his glory did not last for long. It was quickly eclipsed by other more glittering virilities.

This amorous emulation intoxicated Imtissal and created around her the legend of a femme fatale. All the adolescents of the quarter wanted to convince themselves of their erotic acumen, and so her room was never empty. However, at the end of the day, Imtissal was tired and didn't know where to go to relax or to get a change of air. Before the child was born, she often went to the movies. The vulgar sentimentality of the stories which unrolled before her eyes was a comfort and made her forget her own life. This pleasure was now forbidden her; she could not leave the infant alone. She was suffocating in her room and her existence began to seem wretched to her, bound up in distress and loneliness.

She went over to the cradle and watched the baby sleeping. It was strange the way he slept all the time. Even the coming and going of her clients did not seem to disturb him. Sometimes, Imtissal thought he was dead. She had to lean down close over him to hear his thin, fragile breathing. For a long moment she stood by the cradle and watched. Then, she went to her bed, stretched herself out on it and sank down into her thoughts.

It happened now that she often thought of Rafik, but this was only to delight in imagining him tortured and restless. The marriage of old Hafez seemed to her like a divine vengeance. She could not think without a malevolent pleasure of this grotesque event which was going to ruin the life of her former lover. She had never forgiven him for leaving her, for giving in to his father. For a long time she had wished the worst afflictions on him. And now her desire was going to be realized by an unforeseen event. From now on Rafik would be enclosed in a circle of torments that would make him dizzy. Imtissal already knew through Hoda that the young man could no longer sleep, and that he was contriving by all possible means to prevent his father's marriage. She was eager to know all the details of this scabrous affair. She was waiting for the next visit of Hoda, who had promised to bring her news of the latest developments. Rafik's discomforts had become the only distraction that brightened her imprisonment.

Someone knocked on the door. She got up from the bed and

went to open it. In the obscurity of the landing she couldn't make out the face of her visitor. She thought he was one of her clients and said mechanically:

"Come in."

"It's me," said Rafik. He entered the room and closed the door behind him.

Imtissal uttered a cry and thrust out her hands as if to repel the apparition of a ghost. She drew back to the bed, lowered her hands, and remained stunned for several minutes. She could not bring herself to realize that Rafik was in her room. Then she recovered and started to overwhelm him with abuse.

"Scoundrel! Why did you come here? I don't want to see you."

"For heaven's sake, stop shouting," Rafik said. "I didn't come here to fight with you. I've got to talk to you."

"What have you got to say to me?" Imtissal cried. "Get out of here, you devil!"

Rafik stood in the middle of the room, still out of breath from his haste to escape Mimi. The brutal way he had left Mimi, after having wounded his artist's vanity, had so pleased him that he had arrived at Imtissal's room without knowing it. All along the way he had thought only of Mimi's sorrowful and bewildered face illuminated by the vague glare of a distant street lamp. And now, in Imtissal's room, he still thought of the scene with satanic joy. For some time he remained indifferent to the hysterical rage of the woman, then he yawned, remembered he had come to explain something, leaned on the back of a chair and said weakly:

"Listen! I don't deserve your insults. Why do you treat me like an enemy? I've only come to explain to you ..."

"And how would you like me to treat you?" Imtissal cried at the height of her fury. "You who've done so much harm to me! Do you expect me to be grateful to you? Listen to him. What impudence!"

"I've suffered as much as you have," Rafik said. "But it had to be. Try to understand that I've come to explain all that to you."

"Explain what? I know you and your family. All the quarter knows you. You're snobs and idlers. And you dare come here to insult me!"

"I haven't come to insult you. Just listen to me. And above all, stop shouting. You'll rouse everybody."

"You're afraid of everybody now? Don't worry. This isn't a cemetery like your house. People are alive here: shouts don't disturb them. I'd like them to come and find you here. That would be a pretty sight."

"I beg you, Imtissal, don't cause a scandal."

She laughed sarcastically.

"A scandal! The scandal is you and your family. You can't get away from it. Everybody knows about you. No one would learn anything new."

She had sat down on the edge of her bed, her dressing gown half open over her naked legs, in a pose of abandon that contrasted with the hate reflected in her eyes. She seemed calm now, her rage had yielded to the bitter pleasure of fully tasting her vengeance. She thought she understood why Rafik had come to see her. His unhappiness had brought him. She couldn't believe anything else. The approaching marriage of his father— this menace had finally roused him from his inertia. He had only come to her in search of a little consolation—to dissipate the torments that were stifling him. She saw him so beaten down that she had one instant of forgetfulness, and all her being was invaded by pity. But this only lasted a moment. She became enraged and vindictive almost at once.

"I know what brought you here," she said. "You've left home, and so you've come to tell me all your troubles. I warn you, don't count on any sympathy from me. You won't get it."

"I don't want your pity," Rafik said.

"What do you want then, you bastard?"

"First I'd like to sit down," he said. "I'm very tired."

He sank into a chair and sat immobile, his back stooped, his gaze absent. Imtissal had almost cried out again to stop him from sitting down, but she remained voiceless, held by a kind of contagious torpor which emanated from the young man. It was true that the simple presence of these people induced drowsiness, even sleep; Hoda was right. Before the lax and almost lifeless air of Rafik, she was seized by a frightful weakness; she felt herself the prey of a senseless dizziness. She couldn't fight against the sensation of torpor which held her. She closed her eyes as if under the shock of a sudden fatigue, reopened them with fear and looked at the young man slumped in the chair. Before him she felt as impotent as if she were faced with a corpse. How could she fight a dead man?

Rafik had not budged; he felt secure in this room and thought only of going to sleep. The silence which had followed Imtissal's abuse seemed propitious to sleep. Yet some torment persisted in him. The comfortable warmth of the room concealed a trap more cunning than all the traps of the world: the presence of this woman's body, half clothed, swollen with anger and stupor. He made a great effort not to look at her. In spite of him, she was crushing him with her massiveness, becoming more vital and obscene. He thought he would never get to sleep and stared at her with terror. What he saw convinced him of the danger he was in. Fallen back on the bed, Imtissal had spread her legs, and her half-opened dressing gown bared, like a defiance, the inexorable nudity of her flesh. There was no doubt, she defied him. But, extraordinary thing, he felt no desire before that offered flesh. All that was part of a world long since abandoned; it was a pale vision from a distant and miserable past. He sighed, yawned, stretched himself full length, then once more fell into immobility and silence.

"Speak," she said. "Tell me what you want."

He looked at her, a little stupefied. He had completely forgotten why he had come and tried to remember.

"I've simply come to tell you why I left you two years ago. Back then you wouldn't allow me to explain my decision. You chased me out like a dog, without even wanting to listen to me. And then, the idea that you thought I was only obeying my father tormented me. There is something else. I want to make you understand what forced me to act the way I did ..."

"Your father!" Imtissal cried. "I knew you'd end up talking about him. He's the reason you came here tonight. I know what he's cooking up for you, and it makes me very happy."

She burst out with a strident laugh that made the flame of the candle dance. A feeble cry of fright came from the cradle.

"He wants to get married?"

"You know about it, then," said Rafik, stunned by her question.

"Yes, I know about it, and I'm delighted by the news. It gives me great pleasure to see you miserable at last."

"Don't rejoice too soon," Rafik said. "The marriage is not going to take place."

"You're going to stop it, I suppose! Infant!"

"Perhaps I don't have to stop it," he said. "In any case, the marriage will not take place. There's one thing you don't know about."

"What, you devil?"

Rafik did not reply. He realized he had ventured too far. Now he had to tell this wretched woman everything because she wished to know everything.

"What thing? Tell me."

He smiled slyly, closed his eyes, and said after a moment of silence:

"It's a secret."

"The hell with you! What's the secret?"

"I can't tell you that."

"By Allah, you'd better tell me! If you don't I'll scream so loud all the neighbors will come here and chase you out like a dog. Come, tell me, tell me!"

In spite of his torpor, Rafik sensed a storm and searched for a refuge against this possible onslaught. But it was too late for him to react. There was no limit to the fury of this woman. He knew that too well; she was capable of rousing the whole quarter for the simple pleasure of creating a scandal.

"Ah well!" he said. "Since you insist you might as well know that my dear father has a hernia."

"A hernia!" she exclaimed.

"A hideous hernia," said Rafik. "A real disaster."

Imtissal leaned forward and stared at Rafik with a dazed look.

"I don't understand. What is this hernia? You're making a fool of me, scum!"

"It's easy enough to understand," said Rafik. "You undoubtedly know what a hernia is? Very well! My dear father is afflicted with a hernia as big as a watermelon. One doesn't marry with a thing like that. Now do you understand?"

Imtissal remained dumfounded for a moment as she began to comprehend. Then she was seized by a sudden fit of hysteria, and began to jerk as she laughed, her bead thrown back, her body shaking with convulsions.

"I beg you, he quiet," Rafik implored.

She didn't seem to hear him; she laughed on, carried away by a wild gaiety. Rafik stared at her, his face drained by terror. The spectacle of this degraded frenzy brought him back again to a detested world of perversity and corruption. He would have liked to flee, but his inertia held him in the chair, and he felt that her laughter would follow him forever in his sleep.

At last she calmed herself.

"What a family!" she said. "I could wish to kill you all, but instead you'll make me die laughing at your stories."

"This is hardly a story to laugh at," said Rafik. "If you only knew what I suffered before I found out about this hernia. I couldn't sleep. It's saved us all from a catastrophe."

"No matter, it's a charming tale," said Imtissal. "And trust me, I'll take it upon myself to spread it around the quarter."

But suddenly she appeared to be profoundly disappointed. The thought that the marriage of old Hafez could really be ruined by this hernia moved her so that her eyes filled with tears. Her vengeance might escape her. Then anger seized her again, and glaring at the young man she cried:

"It isn't true!"

"What isn't true?'

'That your father has a hernia. It's a lie you've invented to get me in trouble. Admit it, you bastard."

"It's all true," said Rafik. "On my honor, it's no lie. My father has a hernia. Do you want to see it?"

"Shut up, dog! Do you want me to kill you?"

"Forgive me," said Rafik. "I see you don't dare accept it. However, it exists. Believe me."

He was alarmed to see this stupid grief in her. For the first time he noticed the changes in her features. On her face, already aged, was the brand of long prostitution. Rafik felt again an immense pity for her, and saw that she would soon be nothing more than a worn-out whore with hanging flesh. But what was this woman's fate to him? There were thousands like her spread across the world. She could do him nothing but harm.

"Listen to me, Imtissal. I haven't come to talk about my father's hernia. Now, I beg you, stop treating me like an enemy.

You must know why I abandoned you two years ago, and you must pardon me. You thought it was in obedience to my father, and that isn't true. The truth is that I was afraid."

"Afraid of what?" demanded Imtissal.

"I was afraid of all that was not our house. Of all that moves and strives uselessly in life. When I'm not in my bed, I feel as though something fatal will happen to me. I'm not really at peace except in bed. That's easy enough to understand."

"I won't try," cried Imtissal, "You've come to tell me these stupid little stories, you son of a whore."

"Yes. I've wanted to make you understand the distance that has separated us for a long time. I knew you wanted me to leave you. But now that you know the reason, I hope you'll forgive me."

"Forgive you!" said Imtissal. "Then you think I've suffered for two years only for you to come and tell me stories? How am I supposed to believe that you're sorry?"

"But I'm not sorry," said Rafik. "What I thought for two years I'm more convinced of now than ever. All I want is to know that you understand that my father had nothing to do with my decision, and that my sleep is what I wanted to save by abandoning you."

"I don't understand anything," said Imtissal. "You're an idler—that I knew. You don't have to explain that to me. But I hoped that through love for me you'd do anything to shake off your laziness. You could have worked and earned a living without help from your father. We could have been so happy with each other!"

"Work!" cried Rafik. "Earn a living! That's all you think of. And you pretend you loved me. What would you have done to me if you hadn't loved me! You can kill a man with ideas like that. No, Imtissal, I'm not made for work."

"What are you made for then?"

"I'm made to sleep and to live in a corner, away from men. Listen, Imtissal, I'm afraid of men. They're all criminals—like you—always wanting to make others work."

"You're a fool. Besides, all your family are corrupters. Damn the day I knew you and loved you!"

She was still sitting on the bed, and stared at him in silence and antagonism. This man she had loved had revealed himself to her like the malingering touch of a contagious disease. Never had she expected this exhibition of indolence which bordered on madness. She remained voiceless, subdued by fear, wondering how she could get rid of him.

Rafik suddenly felt overwhelmed by a great torpor. He began to be aware of a profound listlessness, and a great need for sleep tortured him. What had he come looking for at this woman's house? An explanation? He should have guessed she would understand nothing. She was like the others, tainted by her mean existence, indoctrinated with righteousness, and ready to overturn the world for a love story. She couldn't remain at rest; she must be on the move all the time, and make others move. He looked at her fixedly, astonished that this woman, almost naked and whom he had loved, was so close to him, yet gave him no desire to caress her. Even the simple thought of caressing her terrified him like the threat of some laborious business. He glanced away, opened his mouth to yawn, but stopped, disturbed by the sight of the cradle.

A strange emotion mastered him. He paused for a long moment, then rose, approached the cradle unsteadily, and stared at the sleeping infant: Imtissal watched him, her face hard and anguished.

"He's sleeping," he said.

"Yes," said Imtissal. "He's as lazy as you are. But he isn't your son."

"I know. No matter, I love this child. He sleeps so well. Above all he doesn't talk of work."

He returned and looked at Imtissal, his eyes half-closed, as though lost in an exquisite dream.

"Let me sleep on your bed for a moment," he asked in a supplicating tone. "I promise — only for a moment. Then I'll leave at once."

Imtissal remained stifled, without strength. She knew she was defeated by this immense inertia which nothing could rouse. She shook with sobs and began to tear her hair, screaming curses. But Rafik went over to her slowly, unmoved by her cries. Suddenly he sank down on the bed, and was carried away by the heavy waves of sleep.

XIV

O ld Hafez was sitting in his bed contemplating his hernia
with wonder and dismay. Each time he awoke, the sight of
his impotence filled him with despair. He put a trembling hand
on the horrible swelling that never stopped growing—defying
him. It was really amazing how it increased every day, as though
it took pleasure in torturing him, in becoming more and more
outrageous. Old Hafez couldn't even believe it anymore; it had
passed the bounds of the possible and even of the detestable.
There was no doubt that some evil being had cast a spell over
this growth, trying to destroy him. Wasn't it one of the children's
tricks to ruin his marriage? They were capable of the worst vil-
lainy, those children. But, even so, old Hafez couldn't imagine
what devilish and intricate mechanism they could have used to
produce this result. His mind became confused in the maze of
this terrible conspiracy. The absurdity of such suspicions, that
came from pure indulgence, didn't bother him at all; he stub-
bornly held to the contrary, not wanting to founder in hopeless-
ness and accept defeat. He was even suddenly tempted to go

downstairs, to tell his children that he had discovered their plot and to teach them some respect. Only the vanity such a move would imply stopped him.

Soon he was tired of looking at his infirmity. He lowered his nightgown, pulled up the covers and began to lament his fate. How, in this condition, could he hope for a marriage that would rejoice his declining years? Everyone was plotting against him, everyone had abandoned him. Even Haga Zohra had given no sign of life since her visit so long ago, when she had promised miracles. No doubt she had forgotten him. Thus there was nothing left him in his solitude but the dismal spectacle of his hernia. He was alone, faced with this agonizing hernia that he felt forever growing between his legs and filling the bed with its incongruous mass.

To escape his obsession, he took the paper off the night table and opened it. It was a very old paper, yellowed, the type blurred with time, giving its news a doubtful aspect that corresponded with his own views of the world. But he had scarcely read a line when he felt tired and started to fall asleep.

After a moment, he was awakened by someone pronouncing his name in a muffled, respectful voice.

"Hafez Bey!"

He quickly opened his eyes; it seemed to him that someone was calling him from a great distance, almost outside the house. He thought he was dreaming and wanted to go back to sleep, when he saw a black form standing in the doorway.

"Ah! It's you. Come in. I've been wondering what had become of you, O woman!"

"I've been working for you," said Haga Zohra.

She was out of breath, and her panting was like that of a steam engine. She immediately began to complain.

"What a curse those stairs are! I'm too old to go up such stairs. If it weren't for you ..."

She came into the room, enormous and flabby, her black melaya wrapped around her huge body. Each time she moved, her
voluminous breasts stirred dangerously. The room seemed filled
by her presence.

Old Hafez sat up to watch her better. The sudden appearance
of Haga Zohra filled him with optimism. He already foresaw an
end to his misery.

"Come, sit down," he said. "Tell me your news."

"Give me time to breathe," said Haga Zohra.

She squatted on the ground, her melaya spread out, arranging her huge body with infinite precautions on the hard floor.
Then she became motionless, resolute as fate. It was the torture
of the damned for her to drag her flabby, swollen flesh around
to these bourgeois houses, where her work as a go-between took
her. Also, once she was settled somewhere, it was difficult for her
to leave. She had stopped panting, but she said nothing. Her venal mind, greedy for money, knew the value of the silence that
preceded revelations.

"How did you get up?" asked old Hafez. "Didn't the children
see you?"

"I didn't meet anyone."

"Good. They ought to be asleep, it's time for siesta. Anyway,
if they ever stop you from coming up, just shout and I'll come
down and take care of them."

"Why should they keep me from coming up?" wailed Haga
Zohra. "What have I done to them? By Allah, I'm just a poor
woman!"

Haga Zohra was well aware of the difficulty old Hafez was
having with his children since he had announced his marriage,
but she preferred to be discreet and play the martyr. Her work
demanded it.

"They know you're arranging my marriage," said old Hafez.

"So?" lamented Haga Zohra again. "They haven't seen

anything yet, and they're complaining already. I haven't pro-
posed a one-eyed, hunch backed girl that I know of. I'm bringing the most beautiful girl in the country. When they see her,
they won't believe their eyes."

"That's not it, O woman! The children don't want me to
marry. But don't worry, I'll be married in spite of them. They'll
see I'm the master."

"By Allah, what's come over the world? Why don't they want
you to marry?"

"I've no idea. They're criminals, but I'll teach them. And now,
leave the children to the devil and tell me what you've done."

Haga Zohra sighed and assumed a funereal air to show her
sorrow at the tribulations of the world.

"It's done," she said. "But I won't hide that I had a lot of
trouble."

"I hope at least that she comes from a good family."

"From a good family! What do you think, Hafez Bey? You
know quite well I'm not going to propose an orphan! By God,
she has a family. And what a family! I had to live with them for
a week to persuade them to accept."

Old Hafez wanted to expose this flagrant exaggeration, but he
allowed it to pass, and said:

"But why? I hope you told them who I was."

"Of course. But the girl is only sixteen. They thought they'd
give her to a prince."

"That's insane!" exclaimed old Hafez.

"That's what I made them see after a week," replied Haga
Zohra. "In the end they could hardly believe everything I told
them about your fortune and your name. Finally, to convince
them, I confided that you had diabetes."

"What did they say?" asked old Hafez, without taking offence
at this illness that had so generously been conferred upon him.

"First, their faces lit up, then they smiled and told me: 'If what you say is true, he must be very well off.' I replied: 'Have you ever seen, O people, a beggar with diabetes? My word! What do you want!' From then on they were for it."

"Very good," said old Hafez. "You're a clever woman. I won't forget to reward you."

"I didn't do it for rewards," said Haga Zohra, a little insulted. "I like to give service. You know the esteem I have for your family. What wouldn't I do for you? You're the light of the quarter."

Old Hafez liked her respect; such deference to his social position he had not received since he had broken all his ties with the world. Haga Zohra's esteem, even though it was soiled by a desire for money, easily satisfied him in a way he had long since forgotten. He moved in his bed, wiped his hand across his face, then suddenly remembered an important detail.

"But Haga Zohra, what are you saying! I don't have diabetes."

Haga Zohra recoiled a little, and almost spilled her ponderous flesh over the floor of the room. She caught herself in time and said, breathing very hard:

"Now what? What difference does it make? It's something that doesn't show."

"Even so," said old Hafez, "it's an illness."

"It's an illness of the rich. It can only make you more respected. Believe me, I know what I'm doing."

Old Hafez reflected a few seconds; he was thinking about his hernia and telling himself that this new and spectacular malady would perhaps compensate to some extent for the repulsiveness of his infirmity.

"You're sure of what you say, O woman?"

"Of course. I'll cut off my arm if I'm lying."

There was a silence. Old Hafez threw off his anxiety, stretched out in the bed, and drifted into senile reveries about his future marriage. The annoying afternoon light that flooded the room kept him from enjoying the agreeable visions that began to come to him. He closed his eyes and for a long time lay lost in happiness. But he was frightened by the silence around him; it seemed full of things that were after him, determined to destroy his newborn peace. He felt the sweat running down his limbs and was again overcome by doubts. He opened his eyes, heaved a majestic sigh, then turned toward Haga Zohra and fixed a cadaverous look upon her.

Haga Zohra had been meditating upon the different ways in which she might draw the best profit from the situation, when old Hafez's sighs interrupted her culpable reflections. She thought she had been detected; her heavy flesh quivered, and she instinctively drew the folds of her melaya around her vast flanks. Then, her elbows propped on her knees, she leaned forward and asked hoarsely

"Why are you sighing? What are you complaining about?"

Old Hafez, with his frightened cadaver's face, opened his mouth, and gave several plaintive moans in reply.

"What are you complaining about?" repeated Haga Zohra. "Here you are almost a married man. What is there to fuss about?"

Old Hafez made an effort and decided to speak.

"I have to tell you something."

"I'm listening," said Haga Zohra. "What is it?"

"You know about my hernia. Well, it gets bigger every day! It's unbelievable."

"What's that? The last time you told me it had begun to go away. What's happened to it?"

"By Allah, I don't know," admitted old Hafez.

"It isn't possible," said Haga Zohra.

"I suspect the children are playing a trick on me," said old Hafez.

"The children! What about the children? I don't understand."

"It's very simple. They're influencing it. They want to keep me from marrying those devils."

"But how could they do it?" asked Haga Zohra, alarmed to find herself so close to evil spirits.

"I don't know yet. However, I have strong suspicions."

Haga Zohra shook her head. The old man was obviously losing his mind. But it wasn't her affair to correct him. After all, nothing was impossible. Those demons were capable of anything; making a hernia swell would be a marvelous joke for them.

At any rate, her interests compelled her to calm the old man's fears.

"But Hafez Bey, the children couldn't do such a thing. After all, you're their father."

"They're criminals, believe me. But it's not just that. I'm worried about something else as well. Tell me: haven't you thought this would be a hindrance to my marriage?"

"Your marriage! What's this idea? Since when has a hernia kept a man from marrying? Really, you hurt me, Hafez Bey!"

"Then you don't think it's anything to worry about?"

"A man like you," said Haga Zohra, "strong and handsome as a lion, to worry about a silly little hernia!"

"Alas, it isn't little!" said old Hafez. "It's huge." He hesitated a moment. "Don't you want to see it?"

"I'd be glad to," said Haga Zohra. "What wouldn't I do for you?"

"Then get up and come look. I'd like to know your opinion."

"I'll tell you right now. By Allah, you're worrying about nothing."

Haga Zohra pulled her melaya around her, breathing deeply to prepare herself for the effort she was about to make. Then with slow, measured movements, she managed to get up. When she was near the bed, old Hafez drew back the covers and exposed his lower abdomen. The hernia lay between his legs, surmounted by his stunted sex; it was like an inflated football. At this sight, despite her reputed courage as a hardy woman, Haga Zohra couldn't repress a shudder.

"What do you think of it?" asked old Hafez.

"It's nothing," replied Haga Zohra. "I knew it before I looked, you're frightened for nothing."

"It's huge isn't it?"

"What are you saying? Why do you say it's huge? My word, Hafez Bey, you're dreaming."

"Maybe. Actually, perhaps it is only a dream."

"Don't worry," said Haga Zohra. "I'm going to massage it for you. You'll see, it will go away in a few minutes. Just let me give you a treatment."

She leaned over and expertly placed her fingers around the hernia. At first she trembled at the contact of this flesh, hard as a rock, but she quickly recovered herself. Very soon she forgot everything that had brought her to the house, her business as a go-between, the decaying old man moaning in his bed. Nothing existed for her but this strange thing her fingers were kneading delicately, that fascinated her with its horrible obscenity.

★ ★ ★

 Rafik woke up abruptly; he had been sleeping on the sofa in the dining room while he waited for Haga Zohra to come. He blinked his eyes, wondering how long he had been asleep, and cursed himself for having failed at his post. What if Haga Zohra had come while he slept? He thought he heard whispers up-stairs. He listened, but heard nothing to confirm his apprehension. He stretched himself, making a painful grimace. He felt tired out; his limbs were heavy from his recent fatigue. He had just dreamed that he was a porter in a station, and that a thin, eccentric traveller, wearing a yellow tarboosh, had given him an old fashioned trunk to carry. It was an enormous trunk, and he

had a horrible time lifting it on to his back. Then he had followed the traveller and they left the station. The man walked
very fast, going down long streets, constantly changing side-
walks, not seeming to care where he was going. Sometimes he
took perverse pleasure in walking down narrow alleys, where
Rafik, with the enormous trunk on his back, only managed to
pass by a miracle. This chase lasted an infinity; Rafik was out of
breath from following the strange traveller. The weight of the
trunk was crushing him, and each second he was ready to drop.
Then, suddenly, the traveller halted, seemed to look for something around him, turned with a deliberate movement and burst
out laughing in his face. Rafik, stunned, let go of the trunk, and
it fell with a tremendous crash . . . and he woke up.

He still heard the traveller's wicked laugh in his ear. It wasn't
the first time he'd heard it, it was the same laugh he had heard the
night before at Imtissal's. He remembered his visit to the prostitute, and felt happy to be free forever of that old, dangerous love.
He was finished with her now. Her memory wouldn't poison the
sure joys of sleep any longer. He had no more to do; he had explained everything. But had she understood? No matter! He had
definitely broken with the past. He would not be prey anymore
to those regrets that had tortured him for two years.

Life was going to be pleasant, if he could only prevent his
father's marriage. This awful catastrophe still called for his constant watchfulness. True, there was the hernia; but the hernia
wouldn't stop Haga Zohra. She was even capable of transform-
ing it into a thing of glory. Rafik knew he had to keep his eyes
open; the least negligence on his part might ruin everything. He
must keep Haga Zohra out of the house; if he had to, he could
beat her, in spite of her great size.

He got off the sofa, walked around the table, and looked out
the window. The sun was shining on the house across the way, on
the perpetually closed shutters. Rafik thought of the women held

prisoner by the vanity of their males and congratulated himself for being sheltered, protected from them by these walls. Because, without a doubt, they would have tried to seduce him with their idiot smiles and their honest whore's tricks. He would not have been able to get away from the intrigue of these females who had no conception of a life without complication or scandal.

Again he heard whispers. And this time there was no doubt; he distinctly made out the noise of voices in old Hafez's bedroom. He ran toward the hall, stopped at the bottom of the stairs, raised his head and listened. He was right to have been afraid; Haga Zohra was up there with his father. She had gotten in and gone up while he had been sleeping like an imbecile. He climbed the stairs slowly, taking care not to make any noise. He wanted to surprise Haga Zohra, to frighten her.

The door of the room was open, and the sight that met him left him dumfounded for a moment; he couldn't believe his eyes. Haga Zohra was standing by the bed, leaning over his father, seeming to mould some invisible object between his father's legs. The hernia! Rafik leaped to the middle of the room.

Old Hafez, without thinking to hide his nudity, cried out:

"It's you, villain!"

"Yes, it's me," said Rafik. "And I'm going to kill this intriguer."

Haga Zohra was holding her hands in the air, terrified and trembling. She wanted to speak, but her throat was tight with agony, and she could only utter feeble cries. Her enormous body wilted before this madman. Rafik went up to her, seized her arm, and pushed her toward the door. Then he gave her a great kick that sent her tottering down the staircase. She tumbled down the stairs, followed by Rafik, and fled like a hurricane through the sleeping house.

Then old Hafez began to cry in a strangled voice:

"Police! Call the police! Arrest the villain!"

XV

Uncle Mustapha was standing in the hall, nervously twisting his moustache; he was being put to a severe test. His brother, old Hafez, had imposed a delicate mission upon him, one very difficult to perform. The problem was to awaken Galal and persuade him to go up and see his father. Old Hafez wanted to talk to his eldest son about the latest events in the house. Uncle Mustapha had not been able to avoid this request, and now he was seized with misgivings. It was no small matter to awaken Galal, but to get him upstairs seemed pure folly.

However, after much hesitation, Uncle Mustapha decided to face the worst, and went into Galal's room. As he expected, he found the young man sunk in a heavy sleep. His face emaciated and pale as that of a corpse, Galal was scarcely breathing, and he looked as though all life had long since left him. Uncle Mustapha paused for a moment, seized with horror at the sight of him. Then he put out his hand and touched his nephew's shoulder. But the light touch had no effect. Uncle Mustapha braced himself again and shook Galal vigorously. At this the young man seemed to struggle in some dream, groaned, and finally opened his eyes. He looked as though he were coming out of the grave.

"Ah, what's the matter with you?"

"It's your father," said Uncle Mustapha.

"My father? Is he dead?"

"God forbid! He only wants to talk to you."

Galal turned resolutely to the wall to indicate that this was of no interest to him.

"Good heavens, he's mad!"

"It's very serious," said Uncle Mustapha. "My dear boy, I beg you, get up."

"Never," said Galal. "Not if it was the end of the world. Tell him I haven't time. Why does he have to see me?"

"I tell you he wants to talk to you."

"Talk to me? What's the idea? Why does he want to talk to me?"

"I don't know, but I assure you it's very important."

"There's nothing important enough to get me out of bed."

It was a categoric refusal, but Uncle Mustapha was too used to these dark pronouncements, issues of sleep, to be taken aback. He didn't despair of victory, but waited a moment, then said in a grave voice

"Your father will be very angry."

"Let him be angry—all the better. Then he'll leave me in peace."

"Listen, Galal, my boy. It will only take a minute. I beg of you, do it for me."

"You want me to kill myself for you! What is this? You come in here and wake me up at dawn so I'll catch cold! You're merciless!"

"It's eleven o'clock," said Uncle Mustapha. "You won't catch cold. It's a very nice day. Come along! Galal, it will only take you a few minutes. The change of air will give you a good appetite. Lunch is almost ready."

"The stairs," groaned Galal. "What about the stairs?"

"The stairs?"

"Yes, climbing up the stairs!"

"Well . . ."

"Do you think I'm a hod carrier? I'd never get up those stairs."

"Don't worry," said Uncle Mustapha. "I'll help you. You won't have to exert yourself at all."

"I won't go unless you carry me," said Galal.

"I'll do my best," promised Uncle Mustapha.

Uncle Mustapha was pleased with his success; he hadn't expected it to be so easy. He pulled his tarboosh firmly on to his head and got ready to help Galal out of bed. But the young man didn't seem to want to move; a painful change was taking place in him. It took him a long time to give in to this waking state; each time he opened his eyes he shut them again. He couldn't manage to keep them open. At last he grew tired and made no more efforts to open them; he clutched at his uncle like a blind man. Uncle Mustapha put his arm around his nephew's waist and helped him into the hall.

Old Hafez was waiting for them, sitting up in his bed. He loomed in the room like a pregnant woman, his enormous hernia thrusting up the sheet. He had assumed a pompous air to receive his son, striving to appear dignified and imposing.

"Galal, my son, wake up. I must speak with you seriously."

But Galal had scarcely entered the room and looked around, when he freed himself from Uncle Mustapha's arms and let himself fall to the ground. He settled himself against the wall, dropped his head, and resumed his interrupted sleep, indifferent to his father's words.

"What a boy!" said old Hafez with a sigh.

"I did everything I could," said Uncle Mustapha. "Here he is. Talk to him if you can."

Old Hafez, looking at the limp rag his son had become,

remained silent for a moment, thinking. He pondered how he could arouse this inert body that seemed to be under the influence of some drug. His decision to marry was stronger than ever. If only to prove his authority, he had resolved to finish what in the beginning, perhaps, was only the whim of a senile old man. Rafik's inexcusable behavior had aggravated his desire for domination. He didn't want to admit defeat to the audacity of that vicious and destructive boy. He had imagined he could persuade Galal to reason with Rafik. In reality old Hafez, afraid of Rafik's outbursts, was repelled at the idea of finding himself in direct contact with him. The memory of last night's scene still smarted too much for him to have forgotten it. His health had been weakened by the excitement, and as for his hernia, it had swollen again.

He looked at Galal in despair, heaved a sigh and said:

"Galal, my son, wake up. You are the eldest; I count on you to establish order in this house."

Galal, contrary to all expectations, raised his head and seemed to wake up. He had just been bitten by a singularly active flea.

"What's that? What did you say?"

"I said that you're the eldest," repeated old Hafez. "It's your responsibility to reason with your brothers."

"What have my brothers done?"

"By Allah! Don't you know what went on yesterday?"

"No. How should I know?"

"Well, your brother Rafik acted like a gangster! He nearly killed Haga Zohra."

"Good for him," said Galal.

"What?" cried old Hafez. "You approve!"

"It's a crime," said Uncle Mustapha.

Uncle Mustapha was sitting in the rocking chair; he shook his head gravely to signify his distress and, from time to time, sighed with despair.

"It's insane," he said again.

Galal didn't answer. He didn't want to commit himself or begin any interminable discussions. He was already thinking of getting back to bed.

"Galal, my son," old Hafez began, "I beg of you, wake up for a moment and listen to me."

"Well," said Galal. "What is it you want?"

"I want you to talk to your brother Rafik. Tell him for me that if he doesn't stop his criminal behavior he'll repent it. I'll teach him who's master here."

Galal remained insensitive to these threatening words. His father's noisy revival of a show of authority seemed perfectly absurd to him. However, he thought it wise to appear conciliatory. It seemed the best way to get this scene over with.

"All right, Father. Calm yourself. I'll speak to him one of these days."

"What do you mean—one of these days? I want you to talk to him today."

"Really," begged Galal. "Can't you wail at least until tomorrow?"

Old Hafez sighed with exhaustion. He had begun to realize the futility of the conversation.

"All right," he said. "You can speak to him tomorrow."

Meanwhile, Serag was rummaging in the room off the terrace. He had thought a great deal in the last few days. His unsuccessful attempt to flee his father's house had put him in an inferior position with his family. Even Uncle Mustapha spoke to him with a certain condescension, as though he were not quite well. He felt like a child who is not allowed out of the house. No one took his desire to work seriously. This attitude offended his rather juvenile nature and was a constant source of torture. He had resolved to show them he was capable of following his plans through, even if he had to suffer poverty and hunger to attain his independence.

Serag now understood that he couldn't leave the house with any chance of success unless he provided himself with a little money. To get it, he had decided to sell some of his school books, and some of his brothers' as well, to Abou Zeid, the peanut vendor. This would bring him a bit of cash. Certainly, he didn't expect a great sum, but the little he would get would help him to live during the first days of his independence, until he could find some work. Abou Zeid, no doubt, would buy his books. In this way he could enlarge his miserable business and, at the same time, become a bookseller, an unknown thing in the quarter. Serag couldn't get over his marvelous idea. Abou Zeid would be the first bookseller in the quarter. That would raise him in the esteem of honest people.

The terrace room was a dusty little shed, lighted by a skylight, heaped pell-mell with all sorts of kitchen utensils, bits of furniture and discarded objects. Serag knew the books he wanted had been put away in a suitcase. He found it hidden in a corner under a pile of empty bottles and damaged water pipes. He managed to free it, cleared it of some of the dust that covered it, and opened it.

He was moved at this memory of his life as a student and the distant past of his school days. These books represented a magnificent period for him. Then the future had seemed smiling and full of hope. The house had not yet become what it now was: an inviolable retreat of sleep.

He picked up a book and began to leaf through it.

"What are you doing here?"

Serag dropped the book and turned around.

"It's none of your business, girl!"

"I've been looking for you for half an hour," said Hoda. "Lunch is ready."

She came up to him slowly, happy to have found him. He recoiled; he feared this little girl more than anything in the world. Her fatal tenderness was an abyss for him, into which he fell each time with despair. This girl, with her obstinate love and her naïve perversity always weakened his instincts for revolt. It was as though with him she was transformed, leaving childhood, to become a wheedling and cynical woman.

"Why are you handling those books?" she asked. "What are you starting now? When are you going to be sensible?"

"Leave me alone. I'm old enough to do what I want."

"You're only a child."

"Ah! I'll show you if I'm a child," said Serag. "You see these books? I'm going to sell them."

"Sell them! What for?"

"To get some money, girl!"

"What are you going to do with the money?"

"With money I can get out of this house," said Serag. "Now do you understand?"

"So that's what it's for," she said. "Cursed boy! So you're beginning this madness all over again."

"I've decided to go away," said Serag. "But this time I'm really serious. With the money from these books I'll be able to get along until I find some work."

"Then you're really going."

She had tears in her eyes. She had thought he had given up his childish ideas of adventure, and now, again, he was thinking of nothing but running away and roving around the country. She realized how much his obsession blinded him. But what could she do? The only chance of keeping him near her was to leave with him.

"Take me with you," she said.

"I've already told you it's impossible," said Serag.

Hoda wiped her tears and became her most seductive; she

smiled at the young man, offering him her lips. But Serag turned away. Then Hoda closed the suitcase, sat down on it, and caught Serag's hand, drawing him to her.

"Come sit by me."

Serag sank down beside her; he was already helpless, hypnotized. He was never able to resist the perverse attraction that came from her young body.

"You don't want to take me then?"

"No," said Serag. "What would I do with you?"

"I'd keep house for you."

"I'd rather go alone. I don't need a woman."

"You'll be afraid alone. I'll take care of you."

"Why should I be afraid? Work doesn't frighten me."

"How do you know? You've never worked yet. It's hard to be alone. Don't you believe that?"

"I don't know," said Serag. "Anyhow, anything is better than staying in this house."

She leaned against him, putting her mouth close to his ear.

"Take me with you," she pleaded. "Don't leave me. I'll kill myself."

In reality, Serag was beginning to be aware of his fear of leaving for the city alone. The idea of taking Hoda with him no longer seemed so absurd. Actually, the young girl would be a useful companion, and her presence would make the hardships of his new life less painful to bear. Still, he hesitated.

She watched him pondering, her heart pounding. She stroked his cheek, then kissed his mouth.

"Take me."

"I don't know yet," said Serag. "Perhaps I'll leave with you. We'll see. First I have to sell these books."

"Oh, I love you," said Hoda. "Kiss me quickly! My master is waiting for his lunch."

In the afternoon, Serag took the books to Abou Zeid. The peanut vendor was squatting outside his shop in his usual position, warming himself in the sun; he was apparently applying himself to certain putrefaction. His gaunt and hairy face was stamped with an ageless torpor. The baskets standing near him were almost empty.

"Good day, Abou Zeid!"

"Good day, my young gentleman!" replied Abou Zeid. "What have you there?"

"Books," said Serag. "I've come with a wonderful idea for your business."

Abou Zeid looked benevolently at the young man, and at the same time, with real apprehension. Above all, he feared being upset, and the rude efforts that characterize certain occupations saddened his charitable soul. He asked timidly:

"What's your plan, my boy? I hope it's honorable."

"It's an inspiration," said Serag. "First let me put my books down. I've carried them from the house."

He put the books on the ground, stuck his hands in his pockets, looked at Abou Zeid and smiled. Abou Zeid gave the books a quick glance, but didn't dare touch them. He didn't yet suspect the role these books were to play in the project the young man wanted to submit to him.

"Explain," he said. "I'm waiting for your good words."

"Very well! Here it is. You're going to buy these books and become a bookseller."

"A bookseller!" said Abou Zeid. "I'm too old, my boy. I don't think the work would suit me."

"But it's wonderful work," said Serag. "You'll be the first bookseller in the quarter. Do you realize what an honor that is?"

"Ah! You think so?"

Abou Zeid was a little overwhelmed by this proposition; it

was far beyond his poor hopes. He had never been so ambitious. All he wanted was to escape his odious mother-in-law's sarcasms. The crabbed woman continued to torment him about his miserable trade. What would she say when she saw him installed as a bookseller? The question worried him considerably.

"You're sure it's suitable work?"

"Certainly," replied Serag. "What makes you ask?"

"I don't know, my boy! What are these books about?"

"They're school books. Very serious books. You don't suppose, Abou Zeid, my father, that I'd sell you obscene books?"

"That's not what I meant. Excuse me, my boy."

He became silent and again seemed to be reflecting. Serag stood waiting the result of these laborious efforts, their true motive hidden from him. He didn't understand the merchant's reticence and began to feel tired. Suddenly, he saw Mimi appear in the sunlight, his hair disordered, looking as though he hadn't slept all night. Serag smiled at him, but Mimi bowed distantly and walked on, his hands in his pockets. Strange, his dog wasn't with him. Serag wondered why Mimi had greeted him so coldly, and what had happened to his dog, Semsen. Then he forgot the young man, and gave all his attention to Abou Zeid, whose inner debate seemed to be coming to an end.

At that moment, a young girl with long braids and mascara on her eyelashes stopped in front of the shop. Abou Zeid asked her hostilely:

"What do you want, girl!"

"It's for Om Ehsane."

"What does she want?"

"Two cents' worth of chickpeas," said the child. "She'll pay you tomorrow."

"Help yourself, girl! And leave me in peace!"

The little girl took the peas, then went off, swinging her thin hips. A few yards away she turned and smiled at Serag.

"What a business!" sighed Abou Zeid.

"Well, have you decided?" asked Serag.

"All right," said Abou Zeid. "How much do you want for the books?"

"Give me what you like," said Serag.

Abou Zeid thrust his hand under his robe, and drew out his dirty purse. He began counting the money. Serag already felt dizzy from his adventure.

XV

It was almost noon when the child turned off the street into the alley. In the first house on his left he saw, bent over the window sill, a servant dusting a rug and he asked her the way. The servant pointed to the spot he was looking for and the child thanked her, then ran leaping on. It was at least the tenth person he had asked for Serag's address.

When he arrived in front of the young man's house, the child began to call, peering through the gate.

"Serag!"

No one answered him. Then, he stepped hack, made a little horn with his hands cupped around his mouth and again called with all his might.

After a moment, Serag opened the window of the dining room and looked into the alley. Suddenly he recognized little Antar, the child he had met two months ago in the fields, hunting birds with a slingshot. He was dressed for summer, that is, he was naked or almost naked. A sort of loincloth made of some filthy stuff covered his sex. His shaven head was now decorated with short thick hair. He hadn't changed much; only the look in his wild eyes testified to a deeper suffering.

"Wait a minute," Serag called, "I'm coming."

He left the house quickly and found the child, who was already amusing himself by throwing rocks in the windows of the neighboring houses.

"Stop that! You'll hurt someone!"

"Oh! I was only having some fun," the child said.

Serag put his arm around the boy's shoulders, and they started walking along the side of the road. The sun shot down its implacable rays everywhere; a torrid heat hung over all the countryside and over the length of the dusty roads. Serag and the child took refuge in the shade of a tree.

"I'm glad to see you again," said Serag. "How are you?"

"Bad," answered the child.

"You don't hunt birds anymore?"

"No. I sold my slingshot."

"Then what do you do now?"

"I'm unemployed," the child said.

He blew his nose and wiped it with his fingers, then turned his head away and was silent.

Serag was saddened to see his young friend reduced to this painful extremity; he didn't know how to show his sympathy. After a while, he asked:

"And your box, have you found your box?"

"No," said the child. "I haven't found it."

"You haven't seen the boy again who stole it from you?"

"He's dead," said the child a little bitterly.

"How do you know?"

"I just do! He's dead I tell you."

Pressed by the greatest need, young Antar had come to see Serag. His diverse pursuits in the field of vagabondage were no longer very brilliantly successful. His luck was giving out; he was reduced to idle begging. In his misfortune he had thought of Serag and told himself that perhaps he could visit the unfinished factory with him. He had no doubt he would collect a few milliemes for his trouble.

He attempted a disinterested air:

"You don't want to go see the factory?"

"No," said Serag. "I don't think about the factory anymore. Besides, it's always the same. No one dreams of finishing it. It's a ruin."

"Then you don't want to work any longer?"

"Oh, yes!" said Serag. "Only I've decided to go look for work in the city. You did well to come today. I'll need you."

Serag had fixed his departure from the house for that evening, after dinner. He had in his pocket the ten piastres Abou Zeid had paid him for the books, and he had no doubt of the success of his escape. The appearance of the child was an unexpected stroke of luck; above all he must not lose him as before. In that unknown maelstrom of the great city, the child would be a much-needed guide. He possessed useful resources; he would help him in his search for work.

"You know the city well?" he asked.

"There's nobody anywhere who knows the city as well as I do," the child answered. "I know the smallest alleys and all their beggars."

"That's fine," said Serag. "I'm sure you'll be able to help me find some work."

"What kind of work?"

"It doesn't matter."

"I advise you not to look for it," said the child.

"Why not?" asked Serag.

"Because you might find it."

"Well?"

"Well, that would be terrible for you."

"Not at all," said Serag. "Listen. Right now I've got a little money. And I plan to leave tonight for the city. Do you think you can meet me there?"

"Where? It's a big city you know!"

"Wherever you like. You choose the place."

The child scratched his head and thought a minute.

"I'll wait for you under the statue of the Renaissance," he said. "Do you know where it is?"

"Yes," Serag answered. "I remember. It's near the railway station."

"Right. I'll wait for you there, tonight, around nine o'clock."

"Agreed," Serag said. "Goodbye!"

"Aren't you going to give me anything for my trouble?" asked the child.

"Excuse me," Serag said. "I forgot."

"I'll get things ready," the child said. "If only I didn't have any debts!"

Serag went back to the house, his heart filled with joy and pride. He was sure he represented a new kind of man—the man of the future—and he was already smiling at the thought of the victories he would score against the abject world of the idle.

That evening, during dinner, he could scarcely control his impatience. The meal dragged along with disheartening slowness. It seemed as though Hoda deliberately tried to postpone the moment of departure. She ate slowly, taking an infinite amount of time to gather the plates and remove the cloth. She moved about like an automaton, with an absent air, a frozen smile on her lips. However, she must leave with him. Serag had finally allowed himself to be convinced; Hoda was going to accompany him on his marvelous adventure. But she didn't seem at all excited by the approach of the departure, which meant to Serag the beginning of a new life, full of unpredictable dangers. Her stupid indifference aggravated the young man's nervousness; from time to time he gave her a furtive look, charged with pleas, to beg her to hurry. But Hoda did not appear to understand.

Only Rafik had noticed the anxiety of his young brother.

"What's the matter with you?"

"Nothing," Serag said.

"I hope that from now on you're going to calm down and not upset yourself with these wretched scenes about escape and work. We can live happily now and sleep to the end of our days. At last we're rid of that accursed marriage! And you owe it all to me."

"To hell with the marriage," said Serag.

"You thankless child! Look at him, Galal my brother! The ingratitude of this child wounds my heart. We ought to kill him! With such a spirit in the house we can never find tranquility."

But Galal seemed too cast down to answer. His head between his hands, he leaned on the table, staring at the plate of food before him with eyes scarcely opened. He didn't even have enough energy to eat. Rafik was used to his eldest brother's characteristic air of heavy discouragement, but his present attitude was somewhat alarming; it seemed to prophesy evil times.

"What's the matter? Why don't you eat? You seem more depressed than usual. Is that mouse keeping you awake again?"

"It isn't the mouse," said Galal, "It's Father. My dear Rafik, I've just had a veritable catastrophe."

"What did Father do to you?" Rafik asked.

"He kept me awake all day!" replied Galal. "My word, he's a criminal!"

"When was this? Today?"

"I don't know," Galal said. "Maybe it was today; perhaps it was a few days ago. It doesn't matter, I'm completely exhausted."

"What did he want?" said Rafik. "He came down to your room to see you? I can hardly believe it."

"No," said Galal. "He didn't come down to my room to see

me. That would have been less terrible. But he sent me this man without a heart"—he nodded his head toward Uncle Mustapha—"who harassed me until I finally had to go upstairs with him. He had promised to carry me on his shoulders, but he scarcely helped me. It was a long torture."

"What a story! But you haven't told me yet what Father wanted."

"I think it had something to do with a murder. He asked me to lecture you about it, and to tell you not to forget he is the master. It seems that you wanted to kill Haga Zohra?"

"Oh! Was that all!"

"I forgot to congratulate you," said Galal.

"It isn't worth the trouble," said Rafik. "From now on that fat businesswoman won't dare come up here. Let her arrange her marriages in hell!"

"We owe you eternal gratitude," said Galal. "My dear Rafik, you're a hero!"

"You're nothing but an ill-mannered boy," interrupted Uncle Mustapha, who, during this time, had been eating quietly, his face set and dignified. "You have done an enormous injustice to our reputation. Haga Zohra will go everywhere peddling what you've done. What will people say?"

"I piss on all the people," said Rafik.

"What a scandal for our family!" said Uncle Mustapha.

Serag feared a long dispute, but Rafik let his uncle's exclamation go unanswered; he only gave a mocking smile. No doubt his success in ridding them of the menace of old Hafez's marriage had made him more indulgent. He seemed to have recovered his calm and was eating heartily. But after a moment he looked at his uncle, and couldn't resist the desire to unleash one last pleasantry.

"Uncle Mustapha," he said, "I allow you to give my father, the title of Bey. He deserves it. With a hernia like his, he could easily be a minister of state."

"How dare you talk like that about your father!" said Uncle Mustapha. "What are you saying about a hernia. You have no shame!"

"Uncle Mustapha," said Rafik, "you aren't going to tell me that you pretend my father hasn't a hernia?"

"On my honor, I didn't know. Now you've begun making up ugly stories about your father!"

"But it was he who told me," said Galal.

"I didn't say anything to you," said Uncle Mustapha indignantly. "You're all spoiled. Your father is tired of your disobedience. He has informed me he plans to leave you alone here and retire to his estate."

"Heaven he praised!" said Rafik. "Is he really going to do it?"

"At last we can sleep." said Galal.

Uncle Mustapha had purposely lied in order to give an impression of intimacy with old Hafez. He hadn't realized that such news would please his nephews, and that it would even arouse their enthusiasm. But it was too late to retract. He tried to save the situation by taking refuge in an enigmatic silence.

"Come," said Rafik. "Tell us the truth, Uncle Mustapha."

"There's nothing else to say," said Uncle Mustapha. "I've told you all I know. You can believe me if you want to."

"How can we not believe you?' said Rafik. "Uncle Mustapha, you're the genius of this house."

"I forgive you for what you did to me the other day," said Galal. "Only, don't begin again."

Now Hoda was clearing the table; they were all getting up to go back to their respective beds. Serag waited and watched them leave, then he also got up and shut himself in his room.

An hour later, he slipped furtively out of the house and hurried down the side of the road. Hoda was waiting for him in a shadowy corner, dressed up as if for a promenade. In the dimness that enveloped her, she seemed shrunken; her face, unskillfully painted, looked like the image of a candy doll. She had been waiting, peaceful and resigned, but when she saw Serag she ran to meet him.

"What made you drag like that?" said Serag. "By Allah! I thought we'd never finish dinner."

"I did my best," said Hoda.

"Well, let's go," said Serag.

"Kiss me first," said Hoda.

Serag kissed her, then took her hand and they started down the road. First they walked rapidly, then, little by little they slackened their pace, stopped for a moment, looked at each other and smiled. The night was clear, and the sky resplendent, spilling over with stars so real and so close that it seemed one could pluck them like ripe fruit. A fresh wind swept the countryside, bringing the odor of herbs and, from the distance, the acrid and violent odor of the great city. Serag breathed this wind of conquering liberty with delight. He felt it on his face; he felt it on his hands, and it seemed to revive him as though he had just come out of a grave. An immense joy floated through him; he turned to the young girl.

"Are you happy?" he asked.

'Yes," Hoda said. "I'm happy to be with you."

"At last, I'll be able to work," Serag said.

He was exulting in the thought of the effort he was about to undertake. He was going to share the destiny of humanity and participate in the boiling energies that governed the world. His life would be sterile no longer. A daring existence, full of the unpredictable, awaited him. He was impatient to get to the city.

"Try to find a job that isn't too tiring," said Hoda.

"Why, girl? On the contrary, I'll look for the most difficult work."

"You'll get sick."

"I won't get sick. What do you take me for, girl? I can do any kind of work."

Hoda reflected.

"You could be a cab driver," she said.

"No," said Serag. "That isn't a serious job."

"It's very serious and, at the same time, very amusing," said Hoda. "All day long you only have to run around in a car. You could take me along with you."

"Be quiet," said Serag. "I don't want to. It's not serious at all. You call that a job; to sit down all day driving a cab. I want real work, do you understand?"

"It's too bad," said Hoda. "You could have taken me with you. I'm so fond of driving in a car."

"What are you thinking about, girl? Let's be serious. We aren't here to amuse ourselves."

"So much the worse," said Hoda. "Do what you like."

They had just passed the last houses and now found themselves alone on the road, surrounded by the vast countryside and the threatening sounds of distant perils. Serag looked at the road in front of him; it lost itself in infinity, a long line of flickering street lamps. He slackened his pace and seemed to hesitate before the enormous effort of accomplishment. His exaltation had suddenly disappeared and he began to feel a treacherous regret in the depths of his heart. The warm peacefulness of his father's house, from which he had just fled to run after tempting adventures was still too attached to his whole being for him to forget it easily. The subtle threads, made of torpor and the inexpressible joys of sleep, held him to the destiny he wished to betray. He had been insane to think he was different from them, and pledged to the grotesque and boring efforts of men. All that was nothing but puerile vanity. He began to think with terror of the evil pitfalls of the great city.

First there were the factories where one must go to work at

four in the morning; Serag shivered at the thought. There were the streetcars, those sinister streetcars that ran at breakneck speed, heedless of the people they crushed. And then, there was the government. What if the government arrested him and threw him in prison? This upset him most of all. The government, his father had told him, arrested rebels. But was he a rebel? Was his desire to look for work and to mingle with working men a revolutionary act? Serag didn't understand why his love of an active life should be considered by the government as an attempt at revolt against the established laws. It seemed very strange to him.

The thought of the policemen made him sick. Suddenly he felt weak; his head was spinning. He stopped and looked at the young girl for a moment.

"It's still far," he said. "Should we stop a moment?"

"All right," Hoda said. "Are you tired already?"

"A little," Serag admitted. "Let's sit down here for a minute. Only for a minute."

They sat down on the side of the road, and Serag closed his eyes. No car passed on the highway; the silence was almost total. There was nothing but the almost imperceptible sound of the ditches, carrying their dirty waters across the fields swallowed up by the night.

"Do you think we're very far from the house?" Serag asked.

"No," said Hoda. "Do you want to go back?"

"I don't know," said Serag. "First I want to sleep for a minute."

"As you wish," Hoda said.

Serag gave a long yawn; Hoda looked at him and began to yawn also. Then they leaned against each other and fell asleep, indifferent to the furious labour of men, under the peaceful gaze of the idle stars.

AFTERWORD: GOD IS WITH THE LAZY

The lazybones attracts all the waves of the sea. "Let me sleep,"
he begs, "so nice and warm under my white sheets and blue blan-
kets." And would you believe it? The sun's on his side.
                                                  —Edmond Jabès, 1945

Fasten a mast to the bed, let the sheets catch the wind. It is
possible that, if you drift long enough on the waves of sleep,
you will awaken into a world that has changed—though who can
say for the better? The Greeks told of the boy Epimenides, who
was searching for his father's stray sheep when he stopped for a
noonday nap in a cave. When he awoke, fifty-seven years later,
everything that he once knew had vanished. Across Crete, news
spread that Epimenides must be particularly loved by the gods
to have slept so long. For Aristotle, he was proof of the impos-
sibility of the passage of time without the occurrence of change.

Christian martyrs have dozed longer still. The eighteenth
chapter of the Quran—and an earlier Syriac legend—tells of a

group of young Christian men who, fleeing the persecution of a Roman Emperor, escaped into a cave, where they slumbered for three hundred and nine years. Rising from their long sleep, they found their beards had grown long, Christ's name was openly spoken, and all of their loved ones were dead. In 1933, the Egyptian playwright Tawfiq al-Hakim dramatized their swim through the oceanic night in *The People of the Cave*. Awakening into a world where they are hailed as saints, the stiff-limbed sleepers find they cannot live in this strange, undreamt future. "We are like fish, whose water has changed from sweet to salty," the saints protest, as they retreat into their cave.

Languishing in a French prison in 1883, Paul Lafargue observed that a strange mania had lately gripped mankind. It seemed everyone had begun to worship what their God had damned. In their canonization of *work*—that vampire sucking the blood of modern society—they had forgotten His sublime example. Did He not toil for six days, then rest forever after? In his treatise *The Right to Be Lazy*, Lafargue intoned a prayer: "O, Laziness, have thou mercy upon this eternal misery! O, Laziness, mother of the arts and the noble virtues, be thou balsam for the pains of mankind!"

Enter the catatonic heroes of Albert Cossery's *Laziness in the Fertile Valley*, exercising their right to do nothing. In a dilapidated villa in the Nile Delta, a family sleeps all day, rising only for meals. The cadaverous Galal, oldest of three brothers and friar of somnolence, staggers into the dining room in a dirty nightgown. Some say he is an artist. "Why are you awake?" he cries in abject horror. His uncle and brothers are gathered around a pot of lentils at the table. The youngest, Serag, secretly dreams with eyes half-closed of freeing himself from the familial inertia and doing the unthinkable—finding a job—perhaps in the factory being constructed nearby. But on his exploratory walks (he cannot help but fall asleep on the way), he finds the rusted heap forever unfinished. Their father, Old Hafez, never descends from his bedroom, yet hatches a controversial scheme to take a wife in his old age. Rafik, the middle son, must keep vigil during the siesta to kill the matchmaker conspiring to bring such an enemy of sleep into their den. Forced to stay awake, Rafik is fighting against the current in a dangerous river. "From time to time, in a supreme effort, he managed to free himself, he raised his head and breathed deeply," Cossery writes. "Then, again, he found himself plunged into the depths of an annihilating sweetness. The waves of an immense, seductive sleep covered him."

"I should tell you that this setting, this household, they were my family." On November 3, 1913, Albert Cossery was born in the Fagalla neighborhood of Cairo to a moderately wealthy Greek Orthodox family of Syro-Lebanese descent. "Certainly it's romanticized," Cossery said in an interview, "but my father didn't work, and so he slept until noon. My brothers didn't work either, nobody worked.... In truth, we were all sleeping. If someone heard a noise in the house, no one would move to go see what it was, even if there had been a thief." Laziness, Cossery claimed, was the only thing his father Salim had taught him. Born at the end of the nineteenth century in a village near Homs in Syria, Salim immigrated to Egypt, where he acquired farmland and properties in the fertile lands of the Delta. While the fields grew cotton, dates, and watermelons, Salim read the newspaper and took naps. Albert sprouted under the wing of his grandfather, who lived with them in Fagalla. One day the grandfather decreed he would no longer leave his bedroom—not because he wasn't able, but because he no longer felt like it. When Albert brought meals up to him, he would find him with a black cloth tied across his eyes, in order to obtain the perfect darkness. Sometimes, his grandfather forgot the blindfold was on his face.

Albert, the youngest, would awake alone at seven in the morning for school, first at the Jesuit Collège des Frères de la Salle, and later at the French Lycée. He began writing his first novel in French at age ten. At seventeen, he published a book of poems titled *Les Morsures* ("Bites"), which lifted heavily from his god, Baudelaire. "I am alone like a beautiful corpse," he wrote, in an ode to *Nuit*. "The first night of the tomb."

Cossery was sent to university in Paris in the 1930s, but claimed he studied nothing at all. Yet he had discovered that being a writer gave a respectable alibi to his inherited laziness. On his return to Cairo in 1938, he fell in with the Egyptian Surrealists — George Henein, Edmond Jabès, Anwar Kamil, and the painter Ramsès Younane, among others. Cossery joined their group Art et Liberté, and contributed short stories to their journal *al-Tatawwur* ("Evolution"). In 1938, observing the growing hostility of Europe's totalitarian regimes to the artistic spirit, the Egyptian Surrealists penned a manifesto: "Long Live Degenerate Art!" André Breton in a letter to Henein from Paris wrote, "The imp of the perverse, as he deigns to appear to me, seems to have one wing here, the other in Egypt."

At twenty-seven, Cossery published a collection of short stories, *Les hommes oubliés de Dieu* ("Men God Forgot"), which sketched the themes to which he would continuously return over the next sixty years: the misery of the poor, the absurdity of the all-powerful, the will to laugh — and to sleep through it all. In "The Postman Gets His Own Back," a neighborhood wages war against those who would disturb its slumber. To safeguard his countrymen's morning sleep, Radwan Aly, the poorest man in the world, fatally hurls his one and only piece of furniture, an earthenware chamber pot, out the window of his hovel at the noisy greengrocer hawking his wares. Even the police are dumbfounded at his sacrifice. Down the street, a washerman sleeps in his rusted laundromat, nary a soap bubble in sight. His head sinks into a basin of slumber, heavy as a stone slipping to the bottom of a pool. Then, "like a diver leaving a wave, the laundryman reappeared once more on the surface of life." He brings dreams up to the surface, like sea creatures.

During the war, Cossery joined the merchant marines and worked as chief steward on a liner called *El Nil*, ferrying passengers—many of whom fleeing the Nazis—on the route from Port Said to New York. It was uncharacteristic of him, this job, yet he would say it opened his world a bit wider. Cutting an elegant figure in his uniform, he seduced the prettiest of his passengers, and ignored the rest. According to an apocryphal tale, it was on a crossing of the Atlantic that Cossery met Lawrence Durrell. When they arrived in New York, the two were arrested on charges of espionage; Durrell protested that it was impossible, as Cossery spent all his time in bed. Though Durrell, in fact, would not visit the United States for the first time until 1968, it was through him that the first translation of Cossery's stories reached an American readership. Dispatched by Durrell in Alexandria, *Men God Forgot* was published in Berkeley in 1946 by George Leite for Circle Editions. It was also through Durrell that Cossery met Henry Miller, who would become a lifelong champion. Miller so admired Cossery's collection of stories, that "terrible breviary," that when the translation failed to sell Miller bought up much of the stock—hundreds of copies—and peddled the book himself for decades. In Cairo in 1944, Cossery published his first novel, *La maison de la mort certaine* ("The House of Certain Death") about the inhabitants of a derelict tenement building on the verge of collapse. "He is heralding the coming of a new dawn," Henry Miller prophesied, "a mighty dawn from the Near, the Middle, and the Far East." Cossery characteristically responded, "Perhaps that is exaggerated."

As soon as the war ended, Albert Cossery left Cairo for Paris, where he would stay for thirty years without returning to Egypt. With a debonair look and an anarchist bent, he floated above the fray in a crowd of illustrious friends and admirers, such as Alberto Giacometti, Jean Genet, Tristan Tzara, Jean-Paul Sartre and Raymond Queneau. At night, he went out dancing with Albert Camus, who introduced him to his French publisher, Edmund Charlot. Cossery lived in a flat in Montparnasse, but soon tired of the constant back-and-forth between his lodgings and the hotel in Saint-Germain-de-Prés where he brought girls. (Though he always maintained that women exhausted him, by the time he reached his eighties, Cossery was claiming more than 3,000 conquests.) In 1951, he moved permanently into the Hotel La Louisiane, that "grim old hostelry known to the bad boys of the Rue de Buci," as Miller described it in *Tropic of Cancer*.

One night in 1952, he met the actress Monique Chaumette over a bowl of peanuts; Cossery asked her to feed him some, she refused. Cossery gave her a copy of his latest novel, *Les fainéants dans la vallée fertile,* and she telephoned to say how beautiful she found it. Flattered, Cossery agreed to meet at his usual haunt, the Café de Flore. They shocked everyone by marrying in April of 1953. Yet married life did not agree with Cossery. She awoke too early. Her constant questioning as to what he would write next enervated him. And he refused to move from his austere hotel room. In a story from *Men God Forgot,* Cossery had described a hashish-addicted slacker named Mahmoud, who cannot shake the affections of the amorous Faiza. "He had wanted to teach her to sleep, to respect slumber, that brother to death which he himself loved so," Cossery wrote, "but alas! she understood nothing of it." Faiza asks Mahmoud how he can live this way. "'How do I live? And what does that matter to you?'" Mahmoud tersely replies. "Yes, I dream all the time." Seven years later, Cossery and Chaumette divorced.

Impeccably dressed in a sport coat with a colored handkerchief in its pocket, Cossery would rise late each day, leaving
the hotel only in the afternoons, perhaps to take in the sun and
watch the girls of the Luxembourg gardens. He would sit for
hours at the Flore doing nothing. To waiters who asked him if
he was not bored, he replied: "I am never bored when I'm with
Albert Cossery." He wrote only when he had absolutely nothing
better to do, producing a new novel roughly every decade. And
yet, to exercise the right to laziness had its own miseries. Forever
broke, he relied on his royalties and income from translations
of his novels to survive. In the late forties, New Directions published the English translation of *The House of Certain Death,* and
commissioned the novelist William Goyen to translate *Les fainéants.* Cossery's letters to his American publisher James Laughlin
reveal the underside of his elegant life of idleness: "My financial
situation is totally desperate." "The rate of the franc is 270 to the
dollar." "I am absolutely fucked." "I am appealing to you to help
me." "Have you forgotten me?" "Send me a check *as soon as possible.*" "I am always, and I continue to be, in extreme misery."
Laughlin replied with detailed instructions on how to change
money on the Parisian black market for a better rate. At a meeting at a Paris café in the late fifties, Cossery complained so bitterly about how badly his books had sold in the US that Laughlin
handed him money out of his wallet.

If he had little American readership, Cossery had even less
of an Egyptian one. On a rare visit to Cairo in the nineties, his
dogged Arabic translator Mahmud Qassim—who translated
and published four of Cossery's novels—insisted on "a meeting
of two monuments." He dragged Cossery to meet Naguib Mah-
fouz. The Nobel Laureate had no idea who he was. Although
Cossery claimed to have always carried Egypt inside him, to
Egyptians—those who knew of him—he had deserted it. As
Qassim said in an interview, "They don't forgive him for having

abandoned Arabic and emigrated to another language." Worse, the other language was French, the purview of a marginalized elite. Like a dreamer in a cave, Cossery had missed the revolution of 1952, which had branded French, once the language of bourgeois aspirations, as aristocratic and elitist. Moreover, Cossery admitted that after years in Paris, he had forgotten much of his Arabic. Beyond the language barrier, his celebration of laziness and his romanticization of Egypt's lowlife held little resonance for a readership actively trying to live in, and improve, the country, while often locked in battle against the state. While fellow writers such as Ahmed Fouad Negm and Abd al-Hakim Qasim were thrown in prison, or forced into exile like Jabès and Henein, Cossery sat idly at the Flore.

At the beginning of Cossery's 1975 novel *A Splendid Conspiracy*, Teymour, recently returned to Egypt with a fake engineering diploma bought after years of "studying" in Europe, sits dejectedly at a café newly renamed "The Awakening." He contemplates a statue in the center of the nearby square. Known as *The Awakening of the Nation*, it depicts a peasant woman with arms outstretched, "as if to denounce the torpor of the residents." In the scene, Cossery conjures the *Nahdat Misr*, the granite sculpture of "The Awakening of Egypt" that still stands near Cairo's Giza Zoo. Completed in 1928 by the renowned sculptor Mahmud Mukhtar, it portrays a peasant throwing back her veil and rousing a sleeping sphinx. The two symbols, of a storied past and a vital present, face east to a new dawn. The sculpture commemorated the events of 1919, when hundreds of thousands of Egyptians across the country—students, peasants, civil servants, and the elite—had joined together in civil disobedience to reject the British occupation. Cossery was nine when the nation gained nominal independence in 1922. Everywhere it was said that, having fallen behind the times, Egypt, and the greater Arab world, was at last awakening—or must awake—from its long slumber into modernity. It was this obsession with the awakening that Tawfiq al-Hakim, a writer Cossery much admired, chose to play upon by reanimating the three-hundred-year-old sleepers from the Quran.

The awakening had at times seemed alloyed with the residue of a strange dream. To transform it into a profit-generating subsidiary of the Empire, the British had introduced new technologies to Egypt such as the railway, the telegraph, and electrical networks. In the early years of the development of the railway, until a steady supply of coal was secured, Egyptian trains, as well as Nile steamers, were occasionally fueled by the mummies frequently unearthed in the valleys. The embalming potions, it turned out, made for first-rate burning materials. A medical journal in 1859 reported: "It is a curious fact that the bodies of the most enlightened nation in its time, many years ago, are now made to aid in getting up steam in the present fast age." Mark Twain, on his trip to Egypt, joked, "Sometimes one hears the profane engineer call out pettishly, 'D--n these plebeians, they don't burn worth a cent—pass out a King!'" The past, no longer able to rest in peace, collided with the effort to modernize.

The stereotype of Oriental indolence, which Cossery pushes to the absurd in *Laziness in the Fertile Valley,* was built into the very infrastructure of modernity itself. According to Egypt's retired colonial governor Lord Cromer in 1908, the typical Egyptian was "devoid of energy and initiative, stagnant in mind, wanting in curiosity about matters which are new to him, careless of waste of time, and patient under suffering." Egyptian laziness, in turn, determined railway timetables and management structures, and became a durable component of the system. It was thought that the Orient did not require the same standards of efficiency or reliability as the Occident, and so a different approximation of punctuality was enforced for British and Egyptian trains. As "Arab time" became institutionalized, the stereotype of idleness became a self-fulfilling prophecy: Egyptians would languish for hours in stations waiting for the capricious train.

If the trains reified laziness, it was the arrival of electricity that gave a jolt to the spirit. For some, electricity took the possibility of an "awakening" out of the realm of metaphor and into that of hard science, as it was understood at the time. In 1905, as discoveries were being made in the field of electromagnetism by Einstein and others, the journal *Al-Sahafa* ran an article on the phenomenon of *tanwim magnatisi* ("magnetic sleep inducement"), and the ways in which the electromagnetic current accounts for different flows of energy between the earth and the celestial bodies, and inside the human body and mind. It was followed by an article, "Are We Alive or Dead?" which argued that Egypt was still under a global electromagnetically induced sleep, from which the West had been the first to awaken. Alert, the West had come to oppress the East. The writer then wondered when Egypt would rise from its own trance. During the rebellious months of 1919, riots targeted the electric streetlights, that technology which tames the night and ruins sleep. The British had constantly pointed to the technological advances they had introduced to Egypt as benefits of colonial rule. As streets fell into darkness, artificial illumination became a political symbol. Streetlamps were guarded by the police.

With the rousing of the nation had come the introduction, not unanimously welcomed, of the clock. (Perversely, though God Himself has idled ever since His six days' work, the first mechanical clocks were used by 14th-century Benedictine monks hoping to keep their prayers on a rigorous schedule.) In 1830, Muhammad Ali Pasha, the Khedive of Egypt, gave France the majestic obelisk that now stands in the Place de la Concorde in exchange for a clock, which some say never even worked. During the occupation, British Time was introduced into Egypt, with Egyptian "slave clocks" taking their orders from the Greenwich observatory. For Egypt to be profitable, it was essential that it function on a synchronized schedule. In the 1870s, the British began to impose the shift from the age-old lunar Hijri calendar to the solar Gregorian calendar. (*It's April 45th*, declared an advertisement, selling a wall calendar, in one Cairo newspaper.) Yet even after the confusion subsided, Egyptians could never fully accept the imposition of European timekeeping. Clock time was not neutral, or apolitical, or natural, as it might have seemed to a Parisian glancing at his watch. The memory of the lunar calendar, something traditional, authentic, and now lost, inflamed the nationalist spirit.

Although it had been introduced in order to further imperialist aims, the fixation on clock-time soon led to a popular obsession with "the value of time." Articles began appearing in the press that gently admonished the lazy Egyptian to "remember that time is money." Hassan al-Banna, the son of a watchmaker and the founder of the Muslim Brotherhood, took issue with this equation, writing in a letter from the 1920s that time is *even more* precious than gold. Religious clerics made efforts to embed punctuality into the system of Islamic ethics. Though the railroads literally ran on laziness, managers introduced harsh penalties for its workers' indolence: half a day's wages would be withheld for five minutes' lateness to work. In Fagalla, catty neighbors gossiped about the Cossery family's idleness.

Against this monetization of time Albert Cossery stood firm. As monuments cheering Egypt's progress went up, Cossery chose in his novels to reveal the deep bedrock of sloth underlying it all. Sleep nibbles everything, he wrote, "like the teeth of invisible rats." In *Laziness*, retired civil servants grow moldy on the outskirts of the city, while in the center, workers in dusty corporate offices are asleep. There is the idleness that stands against work, and an idleness *within* work. There is the private and the public laziness. Abou Zeid, the peanut seller, naps in his empty shop; the factory that would threaten the countryside, eternally under construction, is a stage-set for Serag's torpor. In Cossery's novels, the only one who works hard is the prostitute. And yet, laziness goes beyond doing nothing. "The more you are idle, the more you have time to reflect," Cossery said in an interview in his eighties. Laziness is a critical position by which to judge the world—a perspective the salaried clock-puncher lacks. "The Orient is more philosophical than the Occident," Cossery declared. "Everyone's a philosopher because they wait, they think. Everyone in the West is after money. I have lived my life minute by minute," though it had meant dire financial straits. With idleness comes godliness. Away from the hourglass of the city, Cossery said, "the further one goes toward the South, toward the desert, there are more prophets, more magi—more people who have reflected on the world." After his death, the long-sleeping Epimenides was honored as a god in Crete.

In a cartoon published in 1921 in the journal *al-Kashkul*, the sculptor Mukhtar rides on top of a sphinx, with an alarm clock in each hand. "Did the alarm clock awake you to behold the Awakening statue?" asks a voice in the picture. "It gave me a headache," another voice replies, "all I see in the Awakening is noise, commotion, and discord." In *A Splendid Conspiracy*, as Teymour contemplates the statue of the Awakening, he observes, "she seemed to be lamenting the fact that *she* had been woken up to see this abomination." In *Laziness*, through the character of Serag, Cossery poses the question whether Egypt should slip back into its slumber, given the dissonance brought about by the attempt to catch up with modernity. Serag's name means "lamp," a beacon (or a nuisance) in the darkness of the family home. When he threatens to leave for the city to find work, Rafik attempts to rid him of his illusions. "Do you know, my dear Serag, that there are countries where men get up at four o'clock in the morning to work in the mines?" "Mines!" says Serag, "It isn't true; you want to frighten me." "I know men better than you do," Rafik replies. "They won't wait long, I tell you, to spoil this fertile valley and turn it into a hell. That's what they call progress. You've never heard that word? Well, when a man talks to you about progress, you can be sure that he wants to subjugate you."

As Teymour sits in the Café Awakening, a noisy caravan passes before him. It's Wataniya, the monstrous madame of the local brothel, showing off her coterie of hookers. Cossery's choice of name is striking, for the word "wataniya" means "nationalism." If the peasant woman of Mukhtar's Awakening statue had a name, she too would be Wataniya. The name plays on the tradition of metonymy in earlier Egyptian nationalist novels—such as Husayn Haykal's *Zaynab,* widely considered to be the first Egyptian novel, and al-Hakim's *The Return of the Spirit,* about the days leading up to the 1919 revolution—in which the main female character is used to represent the nation. And yet, in Cossery's version, the notables of the city keep disappearing into Wataniya's fatal brothel. As landowners and bureaucrats are mysteriously killed, the whore "Nationalism" emerges as a deadly trap. Better to sleep than risk her caresses.

Though the people might slave for the flourishing of this new imagined "Egypt," and sacrifice themselves to her, the entrenched powers did not want the nationalist spirit to get too far ahead. When Cossery left for Paris in 1945, the year he wrote *Laziness,* Cairo was in the midst of what would be nostalgically remembered as its gilded age. Money had flowed in from Europe during the two wars, enriching the aristocratic elite. Cinemas, opera houses and villas shot up along the boulevards, in styles that mixed Art Deco with Arabesque and Neo-Pharaonic, a craze that had struck Egypt since the discovery of King Tut's tomb in the twenties. Armenian studio photographers captured pasha's wives in the latest fashions from Paris. A cast of glamorous exiles sipped whiskey at the Gezira Sporting Club, while Winston Churchill, Franklin Roosevelt, and Generalissimo Chiang Kai-shek convened at the foot of the Pyramids. In 1936, King Farouk took the reins of power from his father Fuad, who, along with Farouk's mother, Queen Nazli, had kept Breton's imp of the perverse well-fed. While Nazli performed nighttime séances, Fuad slept with a Circassian servant girl curled up on a rare Chinese carpet at the foot of his bed. Unbounded by means or appetite, the fattened Farouk rolled between his four palaces and yachts with his chief confidante, an Italian plumber, by his side.

Farouk was at best a puppet of the British: much of Egypt was foreign-owned, including its entire tramway and electrical networks. Under his reign, the veneer of "progress" belied the worsening misery of the poor. While the rich literary culture that first published Cossery and Jabès flourished, only one in seven Egyptians could read. Child labor, sixteen-hour workdays, and corruption were common. City sharks swindled the rural poor. As public health improved, the population exploded—Cairo began to grow so fast that it lost control of its own slums. In a short story from the thirties, Cossery described the march of the city lights across the Egyptian countryside: "Strange harlot's body: it spread in all directions, always venal, always interested. And the countryside fled before it, rapid and monotonous. The city chased it without respite. Accursed countryside, which went off to vomit its distress at the edges of the poorer quarters."

In their villa on the outskirts, Serag's father scares him from looking for a job in the city by telling him that the government has arrested rebels. "But was he a rebel? Was his desire to look for work and to mingle with working men a revolutionary act?" Cossery writes. "Serag didn't understand why his love of an active life should be considered by the government as an attempt at revolt against the established laws." In 1945 alone, thousands of workers were arrested during trade union strikes and government crackdowns. It was too dangerous to hope for better labor conditions, or to challenge the monarchy held up by strings. Instead, as Cossery wrote in *Laziness*, "the country slept in its snare."

On July 2, 1952, a few months before its publication date, a case of the New Directions edition of Goyen's translation of *Les faineants*, then titled *The Lazy Ones*, was lost or "hijacked" off a truck somewhere in New England. On the 23rd of that month, a coalition of young Egyptian army officers led by Gamal Abdel Nasser overthrew the regime in a coup d'état. With Farouk exiled, Nasser introduced socialist reforms, seized foreign businesses, and redistributed Egyptian wealth. "Arab nationalism is fully awakened to its new destiny," Nasser declared in 1956, as he pushed for the nationalization of the Suez Canal. And yet, as workers were killed by the police and intellectuals imprisoned, it became clear to many that the awakening had only replaced one bad dream with another. In Cossery's 1964 satire *The Jokers*, a mad old lady has a dream about her son's friend Heykal (perhaps named after the author of *Zaynab*, an opposition leader.) A practical joker and an anti-authoritarian agitator, Heykal and his comrades set out to topple the regime by postering the city with embarrassingly effusive pro-government propaganda. In the dream, Heykal is riding on a white horse and slaying a dragon. Yet after each blow, the dragon is reborn and refuses to die. "And you, prince, you laughed and laughed," recounts the woman. "And I knew why you laughed. Deep down, you didn't want to kill the dragon; the dragon entertained you too much for you to want it dead."

Revolution is futile, yet Cossery's heroes do not mind. Were it to succeed, it would leave them with no one to laugh at. Though he had highly politicized friends, such as the Egyptian communist Henri Curiel, Cossery himself never joined any political parties. "I hate politics," he said in an interview, "but I cannot write a sentence which is not a rebellion." He understood that a mode of living, expressed in his novels and in his daily life, could be revolutionary. In conversation with Michel Mitrani, his interviewer, exasperated, remarked, "This dormancy, it's totally engulfing!" "But it's a symbol," Cossery replied, "of refusing a certain world." Whenever he was asked why he writes, he would reply, "So someone who just read me decides not to go to work." In *Laziness*, as Rafik attempts to dissuade Serag from undertaking such a thing, the slumberous Galal enters the scene. "Why are you awake!" he groans. His brother explains their predicament. "God help him," murmurs Galal. "God is with the lazy," Rafik declares. "He has nothing to do with the vampires who work." "You're right," echoes Galal. "Where can I sit down?"

Goyen's translation of *Laziness in the Fertile Valley* has been in a deep sleep for sixty years. At various intervals, the idea of rousing it was debated, but editors feared it had gone musty. In Cairo in early 2011, I had brought a few of Albert Cossery's books with me. Egypt was in a state of euphoria: by overthrowing Hosni Mubarak's thirty-year dictatorship, it had done what had seemed impossible. Reading his novels amid the exhilaration of the uprising, Cossery seemed irrelevant or, happily, wrong. Yet not long after, following the elections that installed the Muslim

Brotherhood in power, the new rulers began to instate their vision for Egypt's future. They granted themselves sweeping powers, restricted civil liberties, and imprisoned dissenters, in the midst of economic crisis and electrical blackouts. They called their plan—unsurprisingly—the *Nahda*, or Awakening Project. But after the Egyptian army stepped in to depose the new president, it was against Mukhtar's statue of the Awakening that his supporters turned their anger. They spray-painted slogans and papered the failed leader's portrait over the faces of the peasant and the sphinx. In the military's attempt to disperse the demonstrators at the foot of the Awakening and elsewhere, over a thousand people were killed.

In an early short story, Cossery had imagined a battle between the city's streetlights and the moon. "The street was deserted," he wrote. "He saw only the poor street lamp, which was trying to show some signs of life in spite of the intense light of the moon. It looked like a human being, a humble person crushed down by the luxury and power of a tyrannical force against which it could do nothing. In this drama of the street, the moon personified the privileged minority in this world, and under its brilliance the poor street lamps died in their thousands." Rather than imagining the moon as a benevolent orb, friend of lovers and poets, shining above the streetlamp—that artificial, politicized star— the moon is the despotic elite. And yet what remains if we, the lazy ones, have an enemy even in the moon?

We could shut our eyes against the lights. Sleep is refusal, a protest, a weapon. "I am always indignant," said Cossery to an interviewer. "About what?" "Everything that I see." In his first novel, *The House of Certain Death*, the young Cossery had ended on a note of high prophecy: "The future is full of outcries; the future is full of revolt. How to confine this swelling river that will submerge entire cities?" And yet, by his last novel, *The Colors of*

Infamy, published in 1999, he writes of the hero, a charming pick-pocket, "Ossama's objective was not to have a bank account (the most dishonorable thing of all), but merely to survive in a society ruled by crooks, without waiting for the revolution, which was hypothetical and continually being put off until tomorrow." The future is full of revolution; the revolution is forever in the future. The two possibilities cancel each other out, and what are we left with? Cossery's philosophy of idleness emerges as a *via negativa*, a political mysticism of its own. All that's left is to dive into the annihilating sweetness.

By the time he wrote *The Colors of Infamy*, Albert Cossery had lost his voice. Forced to undergo a laryngectomy after years of smoking, he could only hiss. Yet he preserved his routine as ever. He escaped the hospital to go to a café, wearing the ward pajamas. Pushed in a wheelchair by a beautiful blonde, he was as striking a sight as ever. In place of speaking, Cossery would write on notecards in a shaky yet elegant hand, a mischievous look in his eyes. "The loss of my voice gives me relief because I don't have to respond to imbeciles." "To look at pretty girls, there is no need to speak." "I have nothing in common with the world." "I am nothing except what is contained in my books." "Read them, and you will know who I am. All I have to say is in my books." In 2008, Cossery was made a Chevalier in the Légion d'honneur by President Sarkozy. He refused to accept.

Tawfiq al-Hakim's three-hundred-year-old saints, having found they cannot live in this new world, retreat back into their cave. As they lay dying, delirious, they wonder whether it was all a dream. And whose dream was it—time's dream, or their own? "Time is dreaming us," one says to the other. "We dream Time," the other replies. "Didn't we live three hundred years in one night? I'm tired from the dream." Time it stopped. On June 22, 2008, at ninety-four, Albert Cossery died in the room at the

Hotel Louisiane where he had resided for sixty years.

"Men are asleep," he wrote. "Time takes on a new dignity, relieved of men and their eternal wrangles." The moon continues to do as it pleases: ostentation one night, austerity a few weeks later. But the sun, sinking its heavy head into the horizon every evening, is on our side.

ANNA DELLA SUBIN